CU00703807

Dermal

ALLY MARR

Kinkotica Book 1

First Edition January 2024
Cover Design by Just Venture Arts
Chapter Break art by Etheric Designs

ISBN 979-8-9882811-2-2 (paperback)
ISBN 979-8-9882811-3-9 (ebook)

Published by Daphnis
AllyMarr.com

Thanks for picking me up!

Before we get started, let me fill you in on what you are getting into. These *Kinkotica* books focus specifically on a kink and orgasm denial is first. Kinkotica as a series came from the fact that this book isn't really about sex or romance, the focus is on the kink and how these kinksters are diving into it. We won't be getting into the romantic details of how our couple met, nor will we be taking a grand look at their lives outside of their kink. What we will do is dive into their exploration of this kink, and all the other juicy kinks they are going to mix in there.

The safeword is *parachute*, but to be sure you won't have to use it, let me give you a tiny dip into the novel. This is a spicy book, so I get into all the details of what goes where and how it feels. This is a kinky book, so I go into all the details about how *that* feels too. This book focuses on orgasm denial, but other kinks in this book include but aren't limited to (in alphabetical order): Anal play, Bondage, Boob jobs, Branding, CNC (Consensual non consent) Cock cages, Degradation, Edging, Ethical non monogamy, Fucktoy, Ice Play, Impact, Leashes, Nipple clamps, Pegging, Permanent Scarification, Protocol, Public play, Rough sex, and Somnophilia. This book also contains explicit scenes between two men—no cheating involved.

Safewords are used and respected.

Now if that's gotten your fingers wet, turn the page and let's go on an adventure.

Not everyone deserves orgasms.

1 – Caged

David's only wearing his collar and bruises as he steps into the bedroom after his shower. His collar is old and faded; the leather patina turning the sharp black that once stood against his neck softer and grayer. I'm not complaining, as time has turned us softer and grayer too. But his bruises aren't soft or gray. After our last hard impact session, angry marks and welts stand proud against his light beige skin. Pink. Red. Purple. Green. Yellow. Every small change in coloration is easy to spot, and it's all mine. I don't bother to hide my appreciative smile as he steps forward. Hands behind his back, head slightly lowered in submission, and bruises across his body. In these moments, my husband is a dream come true.

A water droplet falls from his hair to his collar-bone, making its way down his chest to his plump stomach. It's followed by another, and another, and I track each one with greedy eyes. He's just the way I like him, and I'm tempted to let him lick my pussy to show my appreciation. Maybe. I don't need him to expect treats for following protocol the right way.

I close the book I'm reading and wait. Our protocol dictates that he kneels next to the bed and ask permission to be allowed into it every night. It makes our bed sacred somehow. Even decades after we started this ritual, I still get a rush of power when he goes to his knees for me. I frown as the seconds go by without movement.

First thing's first: is everything okay? I look him over quickly, tracing the lines of his bruises and deep tan lines, but there's nothing to suggest he reacted poorly to the last scene we had. It wasn't anything very intense for him—it shouldn't be that. His forearms and face are darker from his hours working outside, a near permanent tan from his construction job, but he's not burned. I put my book down as he reveals the cock cage in his hand and drops it on the bed.

This again.

The metal rings of the cock cage shine. David's eyes shine up at me, hopefully, as he kneels by the bed. I can't say I wasn't expecting this. Orgasm denial is quickly becoming David's favorite kink, or at least the one he brings up the most. I don't acknowledge him, not yet. I have to phrase my next words carefully.

Caging his beautiful cock would seem like it's all in my control, but it's not. Not really. He sets the timeline, and he always keeps a key. He sets the limit on how far I can push him. It was fine the first few times we played, but it's not satisfying anymore. It's like I'm a tool for his pleasure instead of being his dominant. He could do it to himself for all the control I actually have.

The struggle is finding the right words to bring it up without shutting the orgasm denial down altogether. I swallow and shift on the bed, staring at the silver rings of his cage. The seconds drag by. I don't hate it, but I don't want to do this again in the way we've been doing this. What I want is—

An idea strikes me.

"No." I finally say, because it's the simple truth. He lifts his head, then lowers it to look at the floor and waits for me to finish. "I don't want to play a game where you have a set number of days to last. If we do this again, I want to decide when you get to finish."

"How long are you thinking?" Maybe David's thinking in terms of days, or even weeks, but I'm not thinking about time. An end date is a limit in itself. It's like scheduling sex instead of letting it happen spontaneously.

This time, I want it to last as long as he can go. I want to see how desperate he becomes in his quest for an orgasm. Especially if he can't focus on an end date. It's certainly pushing his limits, but that's the whole point. After so many years it's hard to find limits we haven't at least touched upon before, but this is suddenly new and exciting territory. How far can he go? How far will he let me push him? "That would be up to me now, wouldn't it?"

"Of course, it would." His voice is soft and deferential, but his shoulders are stiff.

I tap the sheets next to me. "Come to bed."

He rises slowly and doesn't touch the cage as he sits on his side of the bed. He looks at the cage and his lips tilt down. How will he like doing this when it's no longer a game he sets the rules for? Will he truly enjoy this when he has no control? My nipples harden at the thought of having him completely at my mercy.

David won't look up. "Can I think about this?"

I hook my fingers under his chin to direct his gaze towards me. "Take all the time you need. But you aren't allowed to come until we revisit the subject. I want you to think this through."

He needs to be sure because I already know what I want to see: a wreck. What can I turn him into if I do this right? What are the best ways to break him? What's the longest he's gone between orgasms before? It's a record we're going to shatter. I'm going to shatter *him* until he can think of nothing else.

David smiles sheepishly. I kiss his nose before taking the cage and placing it back in its box. He hesitates every time we dive further into his submission, but he's never backed down before. He'll bring it back to me when he decides to take the leap with me.

It's what he wants—it has to be what he wants. He's been submitting to himself with this and soon he'll be submitting to me. Now, it's about what I want. I want him to be uncomfortable, and then continue to submit to my will. I want him to be desperate, and yet control himself for me. I want him to be able to think of nothing else, and yet be able to walk away from the edge at my command. I want this to go on long enough that he forgets what an orgasm feels like. I want him to hate me for this and let me do it anyway.

I thought David would always be a man's man when I met him; working construction, watching sports, drinking beer, and hiding behind his idea of masculinity. Then, to my utter delight, he brought up wanting to play with the invisible barrier he'd given himself. Now he fucks men, he dresses up, and he gets locked in chastity. I think, at first, he liked the embarrassing thrill and taboo of it all. Now, it's a part of him. The cage has been a softer limit for too long, and I need him to surrender this to me too.

He doesn't bring it up until the next day, over dinner. "I don't want it to stay on forever. I understand you don't want a time limit, but I need an end date."

"You would still have your safeword, and I'd leave a key where you could reach it if you broke," I counter. He can still end things if they go too far. He can always put a stop to it. "I can guarantee it won't be forever, but I won't tell you when I'm planning to end it."

Which will be when he breaks, because I will break him if he lets me.

When he doesn't kneel that night at the foot of the bed, my heart races. His hands are behind his back because he's getting ready to ask. I can't tame my smile into a smirk. My nipples harden and my throat dries. Now that it's truly under my control, I can't wait for him to ask.

"Are you sure?" I have to give him a chance to say no, because once he says yes he's all mine.

"Please, Mistress." He reveals the cage. It looks small in his hands. He places it on the bed and kneels. "Please take my orgasms from me, for…" he pauses, and I walk around the bed so he is kneeling to me, "for however long you wish."

I cross my arms and stare down at him. Even in my pink pajamas, this man gives me the confidence to rule nations.

"What's your safeword?" It's a reminder. He can choose for this to end if it's truly terrible. How terrible would it have to be to finally cause his resolve to snap and for him to throw his safeword at my feet in a desperate attempt to come?

"Parachute." David presses his forehead into my belly. I run my hands through the wet strands of his hair.

"Good boy." I grab the cage and pull his hair, jerking his head back. His eyes darken with lust as he stares into mine. No matter how hard I push or how much he protests, he always bends to me. "Get on the bed."

He must know what I'm thinking, because he moves to the middle of the bed as soon as I glance at the restraints.

"You are giving me such a gift." I leave the cage on the nightstand. He stares at it, even as I climb over him to sit on his chest. He only looks at me after I lean over him to tie his hands using the rope on the headboard. He inhales deeply.

"I'm going to tie you to this bed and give you your favorite type of orgasm. Then I'm going to clean you up and cage you." I don't have to tell him my plans, but I can hardly keep them to myself. He groans underneath me.

"Thank you."

I shift lower and kiss him. It's short and sweet and betrays none of my thoughts. "I love you."

David beams. "I love you, too."

"Last chance to back out." I hope he doesn't—I pray he doesn't—but I have to offer.

"I trust you."

Denial

I kiss him again, this time pushing my tongue past his lips and into his mouth. His lips are rough and chapped and he opens them to me immediately. He matches me kiss for kiss, his tongue dancing against mine, sending goosebumps down my arms and stealing my air. First kisses are always exciting, but who gets to live a life where the hundredth and the thousandth kiss is as special?

My cotton pajama shorts are already damp in a way he can probably feel. I cup his face in my hands as I tilt my head and he leans up to kiss me harder. I can't be mad at his enthusiasm, now can I? I moan into his mouth and press against him. There's no rush here. We can kiss until the sun comes up, but eventually he's going to come, and then I'm going to put him in a cage.

The thought takes my breath away. One more orgasm and then he may never have one again. I pull away, biting his lip as I do. He stares, almost dazed, and I can't help but give him another short kiss, and another, until I'm kissing him hard enough to bruise.

I pinch his nipples. He arches into me and I leave his lips to trail kisses down his jaw before biting his neck. He turns his head to give me more access. I reward him with a harder bite, sucking on it to leave a dark hickey under where his shirt will cover. It will make him self-conscious, but won't actually show. I pull back and take off my tank top.

"Iris." David breathes out my name. "You're gorgeous."

I love how in all the years we've been married, he still responds to my breasts the same way; like he's seeing them for the first time and can't believe they're real. David stares at my dark nipples and I can practically feel his tongue swirling around them. His soft open mouthed kisses. The gentle sucks. The pain of his bite. I squeeze them together before flattening them, playing with my breasts the way he would. He jerks forward but stops short as the ropes pull him back. He bucks like a restrained animal.

"Should be me," David growls, staring as I massage my tits for him like we're in a porno. I bet they look huge in my little hands.

Pinching my nipples sends a jolt of pleasure to my clit, and the way he strains against the rope and drops his jaw sends a rush of wetness to my pussy. I'm going to soak my shorts before the end of the night. Today is all about my gorgeous breasts and letting him come between them. I can hardly wait.

His hands twist around the rope and I grin as I swing my leg over him and get off the bed. He can't take his eyes off me. He's beautiful like this: bound and hard for me, with eyes for no one but me. I would call him desperate, but I haven't learned what his desperation truly looks like yet. I will soon.

"Look at how hard you are." I ghost my fingers over his flesh. His cock twitches and his chest heaves. I turn to dig out one of the lube bottles from the bedside table. It's cool in my hands, and I rub the bottle around to try and warm it as I walk over to the bottom of the bed. His knees fall to the side to make room for me. His cock bobs. I climb onto the bed and crawl over him, letting my breasts hang free. His pupils are blown and wild as he stares. I touch my nipple to the head of his cock.

He hisses as if I'd taken him into my mouth, and he watches with rapt attention as I continue to tease his warm hard cock with my breasts. I wait until he lets out another moan to reposition myself. The lube bottle opens with a pop, and I squirt a bit on my chest. It's still cold. I rub my breasts together to warm it and shift my weight.

I trap his cock between my breasts, coating him in lube with small circular motions. There's not enough movement for this to be anything other than a tease. I smirk at him. Teasing is all he'll be getting after this.

"I love them. I love you. I love this." David whimpers. A boob job is his favorite way to come. He'll need the memory for everything that's next.

I squish his hard cock between my breasts and he lets out an elongated yes as he jerks his hips upwards. The lube lets him glide against me. His shallow thrusts are enough to drag the first low moan out of him.

"There you go honey, enjoy it."

The tip of his cock peeks out from between my breasts, as he thrusts up, and I lick his head before it disappears into my cleavage. It's salty with his precum.

Instead of speeding up, he continues his slow and shallow thrusts. If he's trying to draw this out and enjoy it, then I don't mind. I'm planning to do the same to him as soon as I get the chance.

When the lube starts to turn sticky, I suck on the head of his cock. He groans, leans back, and closes his eyes. I swirl my tongue around his head and then lick his slit and release it with a wet smack. The saliva reactivates the lube and I spit on his cock to make it easier for him to keep going.

"Tell me how it feels."

Words surge out of him like I've broken a dam. His restraint from before is lost to a few hard thrusts. He spends the next minute telling me how much he loves them, how soft they are, how good they taste, and how lucky he is that he gets to fuck them. He opens his eyes to watch and then he lets out a long groan.

"Mistress, can I come?"

I grin. "Are you sure you want to?" I squeeze my breasts tighter around him. "Who knows when the next time you get to come is going to be? I'd hate for you to regret how quick you came the one time you could."

He isn't thinking of the future, though. The last time he had an orgasm was two days ago, after an impact scene. He's still buzzing from it. His body still thinks more are coming. I'll let him come as soon as he asks for it, but that doesn't mean I won't tease him when he realizes he should've dragged this out further. Then again, I knew what I was doing when I decided to use my breasts against him. I let out a chuckle.

"Oh, I am so going to regret this." He comes to the same realization. "But please Mistress, will you let me come?"

"Yes. Come for me."

He crushes his hips into my chest and his cock pulses between my breasts. His arms pull against the restraints, his chest heaves, and he lets out a series of grunts as he comes. I won't be seeing this for a while. I try to commit it all to memory. It would be no good if I was the one who broke first because I missed the sight of him coming undone. His hot cum starts to drip down my breasts and I let them fall open, showing him all the good work he's done.

"Please let me clean you up." He stares at his mess. I take a finger to the cooling cum and pop it in my mouth. He pulls against the ropes. Would he break the headboard in desperation one day? I want to find out. Would he be embarrassed? Would he be turned on? "Please." Desperation seeps into his tone and I probably could show him a little bit of mercy before getting the cage on him.

I untie his arms slowly, taking my time to trace the small ridges of the rope against his skin and ensure his hands aren't clammy. He watches me hungrily, but doesn't move. Slowly, I run my hand up his arm, over his shoulder, and fist it in his hair. His eyes close as I pull his head back. I tighten my fingers and he exhales deeply. He's always been the most comfortable when he's in pain. It's a good thing I like causing it.

I tilt his head one way and then the other, relishing the small twitches on his face that give away the pain, and the serene look on his face in spite of it.

When he blearily begins to open his eyes, I pull his head to my chest. He grunts and cups my ass to pull me closer. I release his head and he licks and sucks every drop of his cum off. His teeth scrape my nipple and I arch into his waiting mouth.

I've been turned on this entire time, but the feeling of his warm hands on my hips as his tongue traces the ridge of my nipple causes arousal to tighten into a need I won't be able to deny if I let this continue any longer. I can't help the soft moan that escapes me as he sucks one of my nipples into my mouth.

All I have to do is lean back further, and he'd spread me on the bed until his tongue explores down and I'm falling apart on his tongue. No. If I make him eat me out now he might get hard again, and that's going to make getting into the cage harder than I need it to be. Being a Domme is hard work sometimes. He'll have to continue this as soon as he's caged up.

I pull his head back from me. His jaw hangs slack as his hazy eyes meet mine. "I need you to go wash up, shave, and get ready for the cage."

The last time I tried to clean him up, he was hard in my hands before I could secure the rings. I get the cage from the nightstand and unlock it, turning the cool metal over in my hands. When he returns, I kneel in front of him.

"Maybe we've been doing this all wrong." He crosses his arms. "Maybe you should be the one to kneel at the bed every night."

"You'd crumble under the responsibility." I shake my head. We'd tried on traditional roles once. I could never go back. I dry his soft and flaccid cock with a small towel.

"You're probably right."

I turn the cage over in my hand and glance at him. There's no sign of hesitation on his face. He'll take this leap of faith with me, sure that I'll take care of him. "Thank you for trusting me." I slide the cage over him gently, being careful not to pinch or pull anything. Once it's in place, I slide the tiny lock through the hoops and shut it before threading the key through one of my necklaces. It sits next to a heart charm I've been wearing since high school.

"Of course I trust you." Color rushes to his cheeks as he breaks eye contact to stare at the wall. "I trust you about the time, too."

"I'm going to wear it until I take this off of you." I tug on the cool metal of the tiny key and lean up to kiss him again. I invite him back into bed with a sharp tug, pull him back to my breasts, and give into the need pooling from before. He circles his tongue around my nipple and pinches the other, letting out a hungry moan.

"You are such a slave to my tits." I let out a soft sound of approval as he mouths my nipple, letting my head fall onto my pillow. His teeth graze my skin, sending waves of arousal down into my core.

"I'm a slave to you." His kisses move downwards, and it takes me a second to realize it's because I'm pushing him down. He hooks his fingers in my waistband and I lift my hips. He takes my shorts off slowly and goosebumps follow the path of his warm calloused hands. I spread my legs for him and hiss as the cool air washes over me.

His first lick starts at the bottom of my labia and comes to the top. The second slides between my labia and ends at my clit, where he sucks softly in a way that sends sparks shooting across my body. I let out a sigh and relax further into the bed. He pulls me down by my hips so that I'm lying flat, and then he returns his attention to my clit.

I open my legs further for him and his hot hands settle on my thighs as he eats me out. My chest has cooled considerably, and the contrasting sensations make it all the sweeter when I pinch my nipples. He groans into my pussy. I meet his hungry eyes with my own. He probably wants to squeeze them, but he'll have to watch for now. His tongue moves faster and I squeeze harder as waves of arousal travel across my body. Is his poor cock already trying to grow in its cage? Am I already torturing him? The thought shoots a stronger wave of arousal all the way down to my toes and I groan loudly as my pussy clenches on nothing.

I'm going to make him fuck me without being able to come. I'm going to use him as a toy and destroy him. I look into his loving eyes and I want to break him. I will break him. The key scratches me as my chest heaves with my scream and I come all over his face.

2 – Toy

I'm going to uncage him tonight.

The plaid pattern over his ass shimmies as he washes the dishes. It makes me want to take a flogger to him and make my own pattern. More than that, I want to fuck him, to feel him stretch my pussy and pound me hard enough that I feel it in my stomach. Yes. He should be put to good use tonight. I'll have to be mindful that I don't get him too close while doing so.

His early mornings and my closing shift at Rosie's have kept him neglected all week, but tonight changes that. I finally have time to be with him and he has the energy to be fun to play with.

I trap the key between my teeth. It's been on my necklace since the first night, and while I catch him looking at it, he isn't quite at the point where he's wanting to be let out yet. Which is good—this would be boring if it were quick.

It shouldn't be easy, either. I flip the key with my tongue. Turning him into my toy for the night will help him suffer. How many times will I be able to tease him before he begs for it? How many times can I tease him after that? What kind of animal will all that teasing turn him into? My nipples harden against my shirt, my skin tingles in anticipation, and I clench my thighs together as wetness gathers in my pussy.

My nipple hardens beneath my finger. The water turns off and he grabs a dishrag to dry his hands. His shirt shifts, and I catch a glimpse of his collar. I squeeze my breast. He doesn't know what I want to do to him tonight. A sweet little bunny heading straight into my trap. I lean forward and crawl towards the other end of the couch. He grabs a pot to dry and a smirk settles on my face.

"When you are done, I want you on your knees on the carpet."

He nods and continues drying the dishes. "As it pleases you, Mistress."

It would. I crack my knuckles against the armrest before going into the bedroom. I swipe his leash from the closet and dig into our toy chest, grabbing a ball gag, blindfold, and flogger. The leather is cool in my hands as I walk out to the living room. After I warm him up with the flogger and put my own pattern on his ass, I'll bring him back to the bed to ride him.

My good boy is already kneeling on the carpet. Perfect. I place the tools on the table one by one. He can count them if he wishes. His eyes are closed, and he's still wearing his tank top. I grab the blindfold first and walk over to stand in front of him. "I'm so wet today."

His jaw clenches. He wants to taste, to have me come apart on his tongue, but that's not what today is for. "Would you like me to—"

"No." I cut off his question. "But since you asked, I'll let you smell it." I lay my hand on his good shoulder and pull. His shoulder knocks my hip and his nose presses against my belly button. He dips his head towards my pussy, dragging his nose against me until it presses against my clit. He inhales greedily, pushing his nose into me. I swallow a moan and dig my fingers into his skin. "Good boy."

I slide my hand up his neck and over his collar softly, and he shudders as I grab his hair. He takes a second, deeper, breath. I pull his hair back, forcing him away from my pussy. His eyes meet mine, but they are half open, hazy and unfocused. I tighten my grip, bringing him back to me, and his eyes darken as I tower over him. He opens his mouth but closes it before saying anything. He doesn't have to say anything, not when his eyes tell me everything.

His tongue darts out, wetting his lips.

Would he choose the blindfold or the gag? Is it more important to him to see me or have even a possibility of kissing me? I don't ask. I want to hear him today, and that means a blindfold.

I tie the black cloth around his eyes and then step away.

It's a shame he's wearing his favorite pajamas today. Cutting them off with a knife would be a perfect introduction to tonight.

I trail my nails up his muscular arm and circle around him. He straightens his back and I move my fingers to the back of his neck. His hickeys are fading. I circle the fading edges it with my fingertips. I lick my lips at the urge to lean down and bite him hard, letting him buck as I make a hickey that would never fade.

I wrap my hand around his throat and he lets out a low moan. I like that he can't look in any mirror without knowing who he belongs to. He'll see me in the shower and know he can never escape me. He'll see my marks and realize he never wants to.

I move my hand off his neck to run my fingers through his hair and gently pull until his head turns up to the ceiling. His mouth parts on a soft sigh. Sometimes he fights, *usually* he fights, but he always settles into submission. He wears it like an old sweater.

I return to the table to grab my flogger and I let the leather tails touch his shoulder as I walk past him.

"Take off your shirt," I instruct. He pulls it over his head and tosses it on the couch. I gently swish the flogger and the edges of the tails gently thud against his shoulder.

His soft body tenses. He shifts away. "My right shoulder is bothering me today, just a little."

I still the flogger. I place my hand on his shoulder blade and drop a kiss on it. "Do you not want to do this today, then?" I keep my voice as neutral as possible. I don't want to influence him one way or the other.

He rolls his shoulders, suddenly stiff and tight. "I do, but can we hold off on the impact today?"

"Of course. We can do some light restraints on the bed tonight, but nothing that would pull your shoulder backwards."

After a moment he nods. "That should be fine."

I tip his head up and give him a quick kiss on the lips. After I return the flogger to the table and grab the leash, I clip it onto his collar and let the handle clatter on the floor. His lips twitch up. I softly trail my nails across his chest, shoulders and then his back as I circle him. Then I kneel behind him, pressing my nails harshly against his skin, causing him to hiss as I scratch down his back. I press my breasts into his back as I let my hands wrap around him to tease him. My nail catches on his nipple on the way back.

Avoiding his shoulder, I drag my nails across the rest of his skin until his back is a mess of pink and red marks and his body softens again. My panties are soaked under my shorts, and I'm practically panting in anticipation. He shudders as I lightly trail my fingers over his now tender skin and kiss his back to make the sensations more intense. Once I'm satisfied, I move to stand in front of him.

I lift the leash off the floor and pull it forward and down. his collar jingles as he's forced into my body. "Can you smell it? Can you feel it? You make me so wet, David."

He groans, loud and uncaring that we have neighbors. "Mistress." He noses my shorts, making his way to my pussy. My body heats under his desperate attention. Instead of giving into what we both want and dragging him to the couch to eat me out, collared and blindfolded, I pull the leash up.

He's forced to abandon his nosing as the collar tugs him to look upward. His nostrils flare. I pull the leash higher, and he is forced to stand in front of me.

"I'm not uncaging you today for you to come. I want you to know that upfront. I'm uncaging you to use you like a toy—for my pleasure and my pleasure only." I pull him forward with the leash.

He whimpers as he blindly follows me into the bedroom. "Use me, please."

I pull him onto the bed and tie his arms back to the headboard. "No moving for you." I loop the rope around his hands and then through the headboard. "All you need to do is lie there and stay hard."

"Yes, Mistress." He's excited this time, but by the end of this I think he'll hate it. It'll be all the better for it then.

He lifts his hips and I take off his pants and boxers. The cage shines in my hand. With a twist of the key, I slide the rings off and his cock immediately springs to life. David opens his legs to make room for me to settle.

I unclip his leash, leaving it by the night table as I hook my finger into the ring of his collar to pull him off the bed.

His lips part slightly, but I don't kiss him. No, he wants that, but he doesn't get to want today. Toys don't get to want anything.

I want to use him quickly and be done with him, but I also want to make it last, to savor each sensation as his sweet words and light whines turn into desperation. I'll have a front row seat to the change in him as his desire to please me turns him against himself. I want to see the look on his face as he's forced to hold himself back.

I pull the blindfold off and toss it over my shoulder. I will see the defeat in his eyes as he lets me use him all night and not orgasm. His eyes meet mine immediately, dark as a storm cloud, hungrier than I've ever seen him. His cock twitches, eager to be of service, and I glance at it. David settles into the bed. He's such a good boy.

But he's a toy, and I'd never give a dildo the satisfaction of letting it know it did a good job.

They don't get to speak either. "Unless you are safewording, or your shoulder hurts, don't talk." Fuck the ball gag, there's no time to get it. I don't waste any more words as I climb on top of him and impale myself on his cock. I close my eyes and grind my hips into his because I like the sensation. He doesn't, and that makes it all the sweeter as my clit rubs against his skin. *That's the spot.* I lean forward and place my hands on his chest, using the leverage to set a nice slow pace. I want to draw it out. No fast thrusts, no early releases leaving me unsatisfied.

It's just me and my toy, and I have all night to draw my orgasms out slowly.

He lets out a shuddering breath underneath me, and the sound of his stifled moan makes me moan. My first orgasm rolls over me slowly, leaving me gasping as I clench around him. Flesh has much more give than plastic. I want to leave a puddle underneath him and drown him in my cum. I want to keep him here until the sun rises, and maybe even after that. He jerks under me, ruining my slow pace and causing my eyes to shoot open. My mood shatters around me. He's ruined this. How dare he.

I slap him across the face.

He stills as intended, but the hungry desire I see in his eyes isn't the side effect I wanted. He exhales slowly and I can tell he's tempted to jerk again to get another slap. I clench my fist.

"You are a toy. If you move again, I'll throw you into the corner and force you to watch as I use another one," I growl. I don't wait for a response, because toys don't fucking talk. He doesn't move. He doesn't speak. I grind again, just to show him how much I don't care about his pleasure. He wraps his hands around the rope hard enough that it probably hurts. Good.

I'm wet enough now that it's effortless to shift my position and ride him in every way I see fit.

Soon enough, his eyes darken further. He claws at the rope to keep himself still and quiet. His arm muscles twitch and his jaw clenches as he stops himself from asking for permission to come.

Good. I wasn't going to give him permission anyway.

I lean forward to get a better angle. My skin erupts in goosebumps as I start to ride in earnest, chasing my next orgasm. I start bouncing harder on his cock.

"You are doing so well for me, honey," I praise. I lock eyes with him as my insides begin to spasm. I'm so close I can almost taste it. I moan out as I slam my hips down onto his harder and harder. The bed creaks in protest and I don't care.

My orgasm rips a scream from my throat, and I can't help the string of curses that fall off my lips as I continue to spasm. He doesn't speak, but he grunts as I clench around his cock over and over again. I pant as I come down from my high, and refocus on David underneath me.

He's shaking with need. Desperation shines in his eyes. I catch the red rope marks he's given himself. It makes me feel bad for him—a little. It makes me want to drag this out longer, savor the desperation in his eyes. We both know he isn't coming today, whether or not he asks. David won't be coming for quite some time. I lay down on him and give his chest little kisses.

"You're close, aren't you?"

He twitches inside me. He opens his mouth to speak but shuts it before he breaks the rule. I smile as I grind lightly into him. He lets out a deep breath as he stares at the ceiling. "I could let you come right now, but we both know there's no fun in that." He shudders underneath me but doesn't say anything to contradict me. I stay like that, with occasional grinding, until his hard-on softens inside me. When I move off of him, he mewls.

"Time to clean my toy and put it away."

David sags, the rope gives slack, and his eyes start to glisten. Defeat looks better than a tux on him. I look over his body and cross my arms. I've left a mess on him. Tears swell in his eyes before racing down his red cheeks. Delicious. I grab a hot towel from the bathroom and the sight I return to is somehow better.

He's defeated. Bound, bare, and silently crying—he's beautiful like this.

"Good boy." I sit next to him and untie his hands, inspecting the deep red rope marks on his wrists. "You really pulled on these." I kiss them.

David lets out a sob. I let the praise fall off my lips as I massage his wrist. He's so good. He's so amazing. I cherish the gifts he gives me. He's such a good boy. I gently wipe him down with the hot towel. He rolls his shoulder to make sure it's okay. Then it's time to get him back in the cage.

"That was great." I sit against the headboard.

He places his head in my lap and I gently run my fingers through his hair as his arms wrap around me. "I'm glad."

I can hear the question in his silence. *When?*

"If you ask, I'm going to add another day to it." Am I lying? There is no date I have in my head. I can't actually add to it. Only a moment I'm looking for, a feeling I'm chasing. It'll end after that.

"So you do have an end in mind. That's good to know."

"Is it?"

He doesn't answer.

<u>3 – Beg</u>

My thoughts drift in the cool morning air, but the sounds of David turning the shower on bring me back into focus. I yawn as I stretch, and my eyes land on the paper calendar in our room. David drew a red star on the spot for two Saturday's ago, which is when we started this latest round of orgasm denial, but there is nothing written in today's spot— just the date and 'Saturday' written in bold letters.

It's been two weeks, and I've only gotten to play with him twice. I sit against the headboard with a sigh. I blame work. Every other day of the week is filled with our shifts, and the rest of the month looks the same. It's been easy to lose track of each other, and intimacy, but now that he's in a cage, I'm hyperaware of the time between our play sessions. Both of us have been exhausted, but when aren't we? If I want to play until I break him, I have to make time to break him.

The challenge is finding or making the time to be consistent. If I could wake up earlier, I could start edging him every day and make it a routine. We've never done that before. We haven't done very long sessions either. A frown tugs on my lips. We haven't done much of anything together lately.

The blank space on the calendar suddenly seems like an opportunity. I climb out of bed like a predator. Will longer sessions make him more desperate? Will it bore him? Either way, it'll be fun to find out. Anticipation breaks out in goosebumps across my skin. How many times can he be denied an orgasm before he snaps?

I bring a bowl of ice cubes into the bedroom. It should melt a little by the time he gets out which will make them easier to use. I bounce from one foot to the other until the water shuts off, then I sit on the bed to wait.

When David emerges, steaming and slightly damp, I take my time running my eyes up and down his husky body. He glances at me as he towels off his hair and again as he slips into his collar. The smile on his face slowly grows under my attention.

"Get comfortable on the bed."

Denial

He nuzzles his head into his pillow. "Do we have plans today?"

"Not a single one."

I use the key around my neck to unlock his cock, and he grows to full length in the span of a breath. He sighs into the bed in relief and it sparks sadistic thoughts. How much worse will it be when I have to cage him back up? Will he be forced to think of me often now, every time his cock pulses in its cage or strains against its constraints?

He offers his wrists but I shake my head. Not today. He'll be able to reach down and finish himself off if he wants to. It's not kindness; he'll have to live with knowing he had the opportunity. Giving him the choice offers me another layer of excitement under the surface. What if he's bad? What if he disobeys? How will I get to punish him then?

I give him a few soft kisses and trail my hand from his cheek to his neck and down his chest. His skin is warmer than usual from his hot shower. It'll make the ice play worse. My nipples harden. Each kiss grows in intensity until he's moaning underneath me. I swirl my fingers around his hairy chest and nipple before running down the swell of his belly and down to his parting thighs. He sighs softly against my lips.

His cock is heavy and hard in my hands. It hasn't learned that it doesn't get to come anymore. Maybe, when I'm done, his cock will be mad enough that it won't be able to orgasm again. Maybe I'll ruin David for good. I can't help the evil smirk that I get thinking about that. I don't actually want to ruin him forever, but I could. He'd probably let me. I apply the pressure he likes and stroke him like I intend to make him come.

If he believes that I'll let him, he's lying to himself.

I have to be careful today. One extra stroke or a grip too firm might send him right over the edge, and then this whole experiment will end on a disappointing note. His eyes flutter shut. He's probably focusing on the sensation of my hand softly pumping his cock. Maybe he's trying not to focus on me. Maybe that's him holding back. He's getting close though. Even if I couldn't read the signs of his body, his growing arousal would be clear from the way his breaths have turned into pants and how he clenches his fingers into the bed sheets. He'd probably rip them before giving into the desire crawling across his skin.

I'd love to see it.

I bite my lip to keep quiet. I want to praise him, to let my words encourage him and bring him closer to the edge. I want to tell him to let go of the bed sheets so he's unable to redirect any of his energies away from the gentle way I'm jerking him off, but this is his first long edge, and I'll give him his coping methods. I'll make it nice and easy. That way the next time is harder. I wonder how he'll cope the next time I do this, or the time after that.

"If you beg, I'm adding another day."

When the precum seeps out of his cock, I lean over and kiss it. The salty present is made all the better by the small moan he gives me in response and the way he presses his hips into the bed to prevent himself from trying to buck into my mouth. I meet his eyes and replace my hand with my lips, giving him kisses and gentle sucks and long licks until he squirms beneath me. He's fighting to keep still, but he's failing.

He closes his eyes and surrenders to my hands, making soft little grunts and '*oh*'s as I work him up to his first edge of the day.

His chest heaves and his groans fill the room around me. His cock twitches, pressing into my hands as it pulses. I wait another few seconds, letting him curse as he gets closer still, and then I release his cock. It jerks, bobs, but he doesn't come. Perfect. I move to a more comfortable sitting position while he catches his breath. Now that I've gotten the first edge the rest should be easier to get to. The challenge is making sure I stop fast enough. He doesn't even get a ruined orgasm today.

"I'll do anything you want."

I grin. He always does anything I want—he's not offering me anything new. I slide a single finger up his shaft and his eyes follow the movement as he continues to beg. I circle the tip of his head. His hands twist in the bed sheets again. Now I'm sure he'll actually rip them before this is all over. Oh well, the bedroom could use a makeover.

"I don't want you to come." I pull my hands away and he whimpers. He looks at the ceiling as his chest heaves and I wait for his breathing to calm down. Eventually, his neglected cock limply leans to the side. I can't leave the poor thing in such a state. I wrap my hand around his cock once more, letting my thumb slide across the head.

"Fuck." He moans. His cock hardens in my hands and I let it go.

His hands move from the bed sheets to the headboard and back again as I work his cock to attention and release in turns. He whimpers and twists but he doesn't reach for himself. David helplessly lets me edge him over and over again. My will binds his hands better than any rope, stronger than any chain.

He's hot and stiff in my hand, and part of me wants to tip him the tiniest bit further and let him come. Will it dribble out or shoot up? Will he give me a little or a lot? Will he shudder if I lean forward and taste him? He'd turn into a boneless heap after, more than eager to thank me for his orgasm. If only I could have his orgasm and his denial, to lock the cage in the bathroom and ride him into oblivion. My pussy clenches as my hand tightens, and his moan snaps me out of my thoughts.

I release him and reach over to grab the bowl of ice cubes. I place it on the bed and take a dripping cube out of the bowl. David hisses as I hold the ice over him and let the cold drops splatter on his chest. I then lower the cube to his nipples and swirl it around the hard buds. I move it across his chest, blowing softly at the newly wet skin, and he bucks on the bed.

With another ice cube, I trace every line on his body, every scar and every shadow until there's no way to be sure if he's shivering because he's close or cold. When the fourth ice cube melts away in my fingers, I take his softening cock in my mouth and give it a strong suck. It stays soft and he moans weakly.

I lick and suck his cock until it slowly and sluggishly hardens in my mouth. When he hardens fully, thick and needy and beading with precum, I pull off with a wet pop. I wrap my frozen fingers around his shaft and he flinches. I stroke his cock, the cold and the friction acting against each other, keeping him close but not letting him over.

"Please, Mistress, please let me come."

Finally! Poor man. He's too far gone to realize the punishment he's set himself up for.

"That sounds like begging," I tease. "I'm adding another day."

"I don't think I can do it."

I grab another ice cube and slide it to the spot between his cock and balls. He hisses out as he bucks against the bed, but I hold the ice cube firmly until it melts against him. The cold water travels down my forearm and drips onto the bed and I reach over to grab another cube.

"I know you can." I swirl this ice cube around his softening cock. I'll grant him the small mercy of not being edged during breakfast today. After that, he's all mine. The ice cube melts until there's nothing left and his cock sags in defeat. Perfect. "You've done this for longer before. I think it's the unknown that's scaring you."

Or maybe it's me. I've never been as invested in his denial as I am now. Instead of silent tears, I will push him until he desperately sobs. I'll push him beyond what he thinks he can do, until he second guesses everything he knows about orgasms.

"How much longer, Mistress? Please, I need to know."

"No, you don't." I run a finger up his cool limp cock. "All you need to know is it isn't over yet."

<u>4 – Ask</u>

What was once easy for David to shrug off becomes a challenge as we move into a month of denial.

His shoulders roll and his legs widen as he braces against the wall. I clench the leather handle in my hand as I give him a tease, then another. The tails of the flogger gently caress his skin as I shake my wrist. A little kiss of leather on skin to build the anticipation of what comes next. Is he filling with desire or nervousness? Maybe there's a small bit of fear. There's always trust though, and his posture relaxes. I'm mindful of his shoulder as I flick my wrist, and the flogger strikes in the middle of his back with a light thud.

He's silent. Dipping into the proper headspace for this. I flick my wrist again, and again, until the faintest bit of pink rises to the surface as the leather licks at his skin. There's no rush to it. The leather caresses him softly as I attune myself to his breathing, the shifts of his body, and the goosebumps along his skin. I sink into the rhythm, the roll of my wrist and my shifting stance. We inhale in unison.

I strike again, lightly, but the impact buckles David's knees and bends his elbows. Our forming connection shatters as he leans his forehead on the wall and rolls his bad shoulder. I still the flogger. This is the warm up. He moves back into position but squirms under my gaze.

Is it his shoulder hurting or is he thinking too much about it? It was fine a second ago. I place my free hand against the middle of his back. He flinches before he relaxes into the touch. He wanted to be restrained today, but I didn't want to string him to the ceiling hooks because I don't want him pulling with his shoulder. Maybe he was right. His squirming is putting his shoulder at risk anyway. Maybe the flogger isn't the best idea at the moment.

"Checking in." I frown.

"We've barely started."

"And you're squirming all over the place."

David stills. "Sorry."

"If it helps, maybe we should move to the kitchen and put you over the table."

"Yes, Mistress." He rolls his shoulder and then turns over against the wall to face me. I step into his space and kiss him. He wraps his arms around me and I hold his face to mine. I kiss him slowly and softly, my arousal rising in the comfort of his lips. He spins us. My back hits the wall and then he hikes his thigh between my legs. Even through his jeans, his cage presses against my thighs. I suck in a sharp breath. He slides his tongue into my mouth, and I tangle my fingers into his hair to pull him closer.

"Does it hurt?" I ask in between kisses. I run my hand lightly across his shoulder.

David shrugs but shakes his head. "Not really. I'm just hyper aware of it at the moment. I *can't* stop thinking about it." He ducks his head to kiss my neck and shoulder and I turn my head to peck his cheek.

"Would it help if I restrained you? That way you can't move it much. I could focus the impact on your ass."

"I do have a bunch of fading bruises there…" He hums. He nudges my pussy with his thigh as he bites my neck and I buck against him. "Do you want to make my ass all pretty for you? I can take it."

"I know you can." I moan. "I'm going to make your ass so colorful they'll put it in a museum."

"Mmm, thank you, Mistress."

I bite his neck and suck a hickey right under his collar.

"Fuck!" David's hands find my waist and he turns to expose more of his neck to me. I move lower and bite harder. He groans. I make this mark darker than the last until it's bright and angry and blood red, like any more pressure would cause his skin to burst.

"Now get on the table."

He steps back and pulls down his pants and boxers. I narrow in on the cage. He'd be hard without it. Does it hurt? Is it an unbearable pressure? I lick my lips. He takes a step back, leaving his clothes on the floor, and lays himself across the table.

"I probably don't need the restraints if you stay below the belt." David turns his head to me.

"If you're sure. We'll see how you take it." I let the tails of the flogger brush the table, and he watches them instead of me. I bring them to his side and let them trail across his back. "If anything hurts with your shoulder, let me know and we'll readjust."

"Yes, Mistress."

I slide my hands over the swell of his ass, lightly dragging my nails against the pale skin. I restart the warm up process, with light and medium hits to turn him nice and pink. His small gasps fill me with energy, and I let it out in the next crack of the flogger against his ass. He groans. I hit him the tiniest bit harder and a pink mark blossoms in its wake.

"Warmed up, my love?"

He hums and wiggles his ass in response. "Just about."

"And how's the shoulder?"

"What shoulder?"

I reward him with a laugh and then a harder whack on his ass. He exhales and relaxes, sinking into the table languidly as I pull back to hit him again. I deliver a hard strike, and then a few medium ones one right after another. David groans, low and guttural. It lights my insides up. *Here we go.* I hit him harder and harder to pull that same sound out of him.

"Please Mistress, yes, please."

His fading bruises will be replaced with new ones, and he'll always know who he belongs to. I jerk my wrist to give him a taste of sharper pain, and his groan breaks into a gasp. How can I finally reward him when I break him? There's only one dream of his that I can think to make come true, but the thought is unsettling. I swallow down my nerves, refusing to ruin the scene. It would be the perfect reward for all the torture I'm putting him through—all the torture I want to put him through. But it's still unsettling.

I kiss his lower back and then sink my teeth into him. He yells and writhes. I bite harder in response, sucking a new hickey onto his hips as I run my nails against the warm pink skin of his ass. He wants something more permanent than hickeys, more painful than a caning.

He wants to be branded.

I circle the new hickey. He's trembling already. I'm not even done. I don't even know how much more I want to give him yet. This scene has barely started. His denial has barely started. I trace a patch of goosebumps from his lower back to his thigh. If I brand him…I shake my head to dispel the thought. I've put my foot down about this for years. His complete submission in this shouldn't be enough to change my mind, should it?

With a sharp flick of my wrist, we begin.

Colors erupt on the surface of his ass. First pinks and reds, and then the darker colors of bruises. His groans are louder and more freely given. I pant in exertion. I pant in excitement. What changes here with the cage? Will he want to stop earlier? Will he want more?

He groans out. "Please, Mistress, yes, please."

I love him like this, desperate and wanting. He's barely coherent with need. I'm the same. My whole world focuses in on this moment. I am in control of everything.

I pause in my strikes to run my fingers over his raised skin, and it's electric. I did this. He moans under me and it sings in my soul.

We could be anywhere, my David and I, as long as he is always on the receiving end of my blows. He belongs there. His ass is an art piece I'm not done creating. My palette of bright and beautiful colors mixes with his dark and guttural sounds to create a masterpiece. I'm the conductor.

I swing again, and again. We aren't in our apartment anymore. We're in a space that's just him and me. I exist only in the heartbeats between thuds of the flogger. He moans in pain, and his voice hitches in beautiful brokenness.

I still my flogger. I trail my fingers along the burning hot skin and leave sloppy open mouthed kisses on his ass. I drag my nails down his back to distract him from the pain but he whimpers and pushes his body towards me. I run my hands down his sides, drawing moans like a practiced artist, earning shivers like the frozen winter winds. Like this, I am everything I want to be, everything he needs.

"More." He begs with a broken voice. I instinctively reach for the flogger.

"Are you sure?" I check in. "I've given you quite the beating."

"Please."

I pull back and leave my other hand on the swell of his ass. For a minute, the whole world exists in that one small space of contact.

He cries out at the next strike. It's loud and echoes through the apartment. It pulses in my clit. *Yes!* I moan out with him. It only takes a few strikes after that for him to break. He breaks like a dam, with a flood of tears and a groan that booms in the space. I drop the flogger onto the table as I lean over him and words of praise flood through me.

He is my good boy; my everything.

He sinks to his knees on the floor, and I follow him down until he puts his head in my lap. He sobs as I run my fingers through his hair. Impact always brings out a different side of my David, a softer side. Sometimes, it's the only way to get him to talk about his feelings or confess something.

"You can ask," I allow.

David's fingers dig into my back as he presses his head further into my stomach. "When?" He doesn't even look up from my stomach, and that's how I know he's not expecting a real answer.

"Soon." I'm lying. I have no idea how soon it will be; only that I won't stop until this breaks him. We're not even close.

5 – <u>Safeword</u>

David's been extra attentive lately.

With his orgasm off the table, mine seem to be the only thing on his mind. He's insatiable. He'd licked and fingered me to completion twice before I even got out of bed this morning. He went to his knees again once I brought the plugs out, and I tingled with the aftershocks of orgasm until I bent him over the table.

Even now, I'm riding high on endorphins. I circle his asshole with the tip of his plug. He shivers against it, but he's ready. I slide the plug all the way into his ass. He was easy to prepare today, and he took the first and second plug with ease and excitement.

David pushes against me impatiently, but the plug in his ass isn't going any deeper; isn't going to make him any fuller. There's one plug left for him, and the purple bulbous thing sits proudly on the table next to the towel and lube bottle. I was optimistic when I laid it out, and I'm pleased we've worked our way up to it.

"I think you're ready for The Monster now, don't you?" I tug on the base of his current plug, and he moans. The Monster isn't as big as some of the ones we'd seen online, but he'd called it a monster when it arrived in the mail, and the name stuck. It's rare that we get to use it, since most times we try he comes before we get there. Now, with his cock locked up and unable to get hard, it looks like there's a chance.

"Give me. Give me more."

I liberally apply lube to The Monster, but at this point almost everything is covered in it. The purple silicone shines when I'm done. I push David's plug in the tiniest bit further into his ass and then tug it out. It comes so easily it almost slips out of my hand. He whines at the emptiness.

"Here it comes."

I place my hand on his hip, keeping him still as I slowly line up the tip of the big purple plug and start to push it in. He hums under me. I go half an inch at a time, stretching him slowly and carefully, mindful of every hitch in his voice and movement of his hips. There's almost no resistance and the plug begins to disappear into him. He moans as he clenches around it.

"God, please, *please*, I need more, fuck, I need, ah, please."

I don't know what he's begging for that isn't an orgasm, but I like the desperation all the same. I bite his shoulder and push the plug in a little more just to make him mewl. David looks like a wreck, and I love it. He doesn't get this way when he's in my mouth or hands or pussy—only when I'm in him like this. The plug isn't fully in yet, but I pull it halfway out and then slide it back in. David would be embarrassed at the high pitched whines he's making if he had any mind left to think of such things.

"Can you take it for me? Hmm? That's a good boy," I praise as I continue to slowly fill him with the plug.

"Yes, yes!" he moans out. I start pumping him slowly with half of the plug he's taken already and he rocks his hips in time with my movements. "Give me everything, please, please. I can take it."

I settle the plug at half, and then slowly slide it in further, letting him take the second bulb with a low drawn out moan.

"Fuck…" He groans out the word when I push the plug in. His ass stretches around it the way it had my fingers and the warm up plugs, until it clenches around the slightly thinner neck. He can't handle it for a long time, but it's the biggest he can take. I lean over him and kiss the skin on his back that I can reach. He pushes against my hand, grinding against the plug and a groan rips from his throat. I let him grind against my hand and then I pull the plug out a tiny bit. His next groan stutters into a cry.

My head warms as my focus narrows to the inch of movement back and forth that sends David into a desperate frenzy. He bucks against the table, but his cock can't get any friction in his cage. He can't even get hard. It makes him wilder. It makes me wilder.

"More!" He desperately pushes back against me, practically fucking himself on the plug. He smacks himself into the table, writhing.

"Shh." I try to slow him down, to make this last a little longer, but he doesn't listen.

I pull the plug most of the way out and then let his ass greedily suck the first bulb back in. Instead of a moan, he lets out a strangled groan. I give him a few seconds to breathe through it. He reaches out to grab the edge of the table and pushes his ass towards me.

"You're doing so well," I praise and start to push the second bulb back in, but he leans away from me. His arm swings backwards as he smacks mine.

"Parachute," he grits out.

Instantly alert, I pull my hands away. He's not bleeding. He's not falling. He's not moving. Did I hurt him? Tension tightens my shoulders and sends my pulse skittering. I trace his body with my eyes but nothing stands out to me. Is he okay? I need to make sure he's okay.

"David?"

"I can't do this." His voice is rough as he growls. My throat tightens. He's still bent over the table. His hand clenches around the edge of it and the other hangs off from where he smacked me. The plug hangs halfway out of his ass, and it could be funny if I wasn't worried.

"Okay, okay, we're done," I soothe. "Should I take the plug out?" I ask, keeping my voice calm and level even as my pulse skyrockets. *Have I hurt him?* The question keeps repeating in my head.

"Please." His voice scrapes on gravel, painful and raw. I place my hand on the small of his back and gently pull the plug the rest of the way out. It pops out and he lets out a pained groan. David sinks into the table. There isn't any blood on the plug, but that doesn't mean he's not hurt.

A million questions jump to the tip of my tongue but I take a deep breath and ask one. "Are you hurt?"

His voice cracks. "No."

One more.

"Do you want to take the cage off?"

"No. Give me a minute."

I want to do much more than that, but all I can do is give him that minute and be here. I place the plug on a nearby towel and wipe my hands. All the softness, the openness, the connection, it's all gone. I clench my fist to stop from touching him. I'd hate to make it worse. He takes a few deep breaths with his forehead on the table. He shifts on his feet as he lets out a shuddering exhale and I'm crushed in the tension.

"Do you want me to let you out of the cage?" I ask again after a moment. David shakes his head, but doesn't lift it from the table. "You safeworded," I press, very gently.

"I know." He sighs out and then scratches the back of his head with both hands. "I'm fine. I'm good. You didn't hurt me."

Relief fills me like a breath of fresh air. I move closer, rubbing my hand up and down his back. "Okay, we can fix anything else. Do you want to talk to me now or do you want a bath?"

"We can talk." David pushes up from the table and turns over to face me. He's in nothing but the cage, but my eyes can't leave his face. "It isn't the cage. It isn't *just* the cage. The cage and the plug and..." He sighs and runs his hand through his beard. "It doesn't hurt, but I was throbbing, and kept feeling it holding me. Everything felt amazing but I couldn't *go* anywhere. I just felt trapped and then the room got smaller and smaller and I couldn't breathe anymore."

"Do you need it off?" I reach for my key, glancing at his slightly swollen cock but he shakes his head.

"No." He grabs my hand as he steps into my space, and brings my hand up to kiss my knuckles. It's extra sweet, and I give his small smile one in return. "It's better now."

"Are you sure?" I lift our hands to pepper kisses on his hand.

"I'm sure." David releases my hand to pull me closer for a hug and he squeezes me tightly as I rub my hands up and down his back. I kiss the skin on his chest that I can reach as I listen to his heartbeat. I take a deep breath with him, and tension eases out of me with each heartbeat until he pulls back. "I think it was everything at once."

I can't stand not touching him. I grab his wrist in my hand. "So the cage and anal together is too much?"

David shakes his head. He leans back into the table. He tugs on my hand, pulling me to stand between his legs. "It was fun. We should try again."

A laugh bubbles out of me, but I can't tell if its nerves. "Should we?"

Silence fills the room for a moment, but the tension fades.

"We need another safeword." He says, once the world seems right again. "One that means I'm out of the current spot, but I don't want out of the cage."

Is that how it is? "I admire your determination."

"That way I won't have to use 'parachute' again." The challenge in his tone ignites my insides.

"I will keep you in that cage for the rest of your life," I threaten, but my face breaks out into a grin.

"If it pleases you." He's genuine and yet calling my bluff. How much more of this can he handle? Does he think I'm cruel yet? Is he still trying to figure out when I'll finally let him come? He looks into my eyes, but he won't find the answers there. I don't have any for him.

David's lips take mine with gusto, and I wrap my arms around him as he deepens the kiss. His tongue feels like home and this kiss tastes better than I've ever remembered his kiss to be. A moan escapes me as his calloused hands slip under my shirt, leaving trails of warmth across my back. David squeezes me, lifting me to my toes, and I grin as I capture his lips again.

Married life gets stagnant sometimes. We both have jobs and goals and know so much about each other that there are no more secrets to uncover. This feels shiny and new, like layers of him that I get to pull back, one at a time, until David's a new man in front of me. I moan again, pulling him closer to me.

The unknown is provocative, and I'm hooked.

6 – Torture

As soon as the door opens, Thorn meets my eyes and grins. "What a sight for sore eyes."

It's been a few months since Thorn had us over for drinks at his new apartment. I would've reached out sooner, except the last time we met him…

I hug him, and he leans down to kiss my cheek before releasing me. "I've missed you too, honey."

Thorn looks the same as always and I rub his patchy beard with a laugh. It's almost as bad as his bald head. He shoves me away and then flips me off, but his grin stays. He looks amazing compared to the first time I saw him: sitting outside Rosie's high on heroin.

Denial

He offers me the tablet to sign in. "Here for the night or do you need help with anything?"

While we were over at Thorn's apartment, having a housewarming dinner, David asked me to talk to Thorn about branding. After years of him hinting at a more permanent way to show his devotion, our conversations were becoming circular and argumentative. He thought an outside opinion would sway me, that it would *help*.

As if talking to Thorn would take branding from a hard limit to a reality. It didn't matter that Thorn has been branding people for years now, or that there's no one I'd trust with David more. It just wasn't something I wanted.

We don't dabble in knife play or fireplay. Neither of us have tattoos. He doesn't even wear his wedding ring every day. How could I ever justify permanently scarring him? How could we jump from nothing to branding? Why weren't the temporary marks of a beating or hickey enough?

I couldn't stand him pushing me on it, and we'd argued on the way home and for days after. He hasn't brought it up since.

Would he have, if I hadn't shut him down so completely? David's been so good—

"Iris?"

I grab the tablet sheepishly as a blush works its way up my neck. "Sorry." I enter my information on the tablet. "How's the shop?"

"Busy. My clients are picking up a lot. I shouldn't complain about having more work, and I'm not, but it's enough that I'm wondering if I still need to work here."

Even though we don't come to The Playhouse that much anymore, it's weird to imagine Thorn leaving. "So you can't squeeze me in for a full sleeve tomorrow?"

Thorn throws his head back, laughing, and we pass the next ten minutes in easy conversation. Eventually, I promise to call, mention that David will be by later, and make my way down the hall.

I haven't been to the Playhouse in months, but it's still the same as the last time I was here. The swinger's club is full of the same regulars and the occasional bright eyed newbie. It's got the same songs on repeat, the same dim lighting, and the faint scent of sex that never leaves the air.

David will be coming after work—directly after work—and I hope to have everything ready by then. I drop off my phone in the lockers and make my way down the familiar hall. I recognize the young man I'm here for instantly.

Denial

His shoulders are broad but not overly muscular, and the red shirt button up fits him perfectly. So do his dark black jeans. He's wearing shiny shoes—which David would tell me means he makes more money than he should. His head is shaved with neat lines, and from this angle I can see the softness of his smooth jawline. He's taller than my husband which is good. David will be intimidated by him, even before I make him take his cock.

"Alex?" I ask, just to be sure.

He turns to face me and he looks way too put together to be in this club right now. He probably strode in here from a fancy white collar job. His bright brown eyes light up as he beams at me and he sticks his hand out for a handshake. I can't help but smile as I take it.

"Are you Iris?" His hands are impossibly warm, his shirt has the first two buttons undone, and his sleeves are folded at his elbow. I'm already wet thinking about this man fucking my David. This is the kind of pristine man that intimidates him. The kind of man comfortable enough in his masculinity to take care of himself, put cologne on, and get a manicure. I bet he's all prim and proper underneath his jeans as well. I bet he went to college.

"It's nice to meet you. David's coming later. Is there anything you want to go over before he gets here?"

"I think I've got a good idea of what you're looking for."

I insist on talking through it anyway, and he's an attentive listener. I'm glad he'll be helping us with this tonight. We grab a room by the shower and I bring a chair into it. I can watch and direct the show from there. By the time we make our way back down to our original spot, I think I've got a pretty good idea of how to make this worthwhile for him.

I told David to expect some rough sex, but I'm still hoping we are thinking about different things. The look on his face when he realizes it won't be me getting fucked will be glorious. Maybe he'll think that I'll let him come with Alex's cock in him, but I wouldn't let anyone else give him his orgasm, not after all the work I've put into edging him each and every day. He's not even close to breaking the way I need him to before this ends.

"Mistress?"

David's still in his work clothes: his baggy dirty jeans and sweaty work shirt. He's got his backpack over his shoulder and his right hand has fresh scabs on it.

I turn to him with a bit of a smirk. Alex crosses his arms. David looks at us and his Adam's apple bobs. He takes in the way we match, the smart way we've dressed, and the fact that he's the odd one out at the moment.

He stammers out a hello to Alex and can barely look me in the eye. Perfect. I dressed up for this exact reaction.

"Hi, David. I think you'd better make use of the shower upstairs to make yourself presentable."

"Yes, Mistress." He glances around.

"Undress here please, I don't need you dragging that dirt all over The Playhouse."

His sharp gasp sends goosebumps crawling up my arm. He looks at me with wide eyes. I imagine he's working out that anyone who cares to look will see him standing there in front of us, covered in dirt and sweat, with nothing but a cage on. He'll look like he doesn't belong here with us, like he's the one Alex and I are entertaining for the night. He's desperate enough to undress but not turned on enough to not care. Maybe I'll make him kneel before leaving us.

Are you humiliated yet? I won't ask. He hasn't done this before. It's not a limit, but it's not a comfortable spot for him. I plan to push him tonight but I'll see how well he does before pushing him forward.

David stands dumbstruck in front of us. This must be harder for him than I thought. His indecision is clear in the tight way he grabs the strap of his bag. If he grabs it hard enough, maybe he'll rip open his scabs.

"Would it make you feel better if I got naked too?" Alex offers with a raised brow and a sly smile. David flinches and I jerk my head to look at Alex. There's an easy confidence about him as he meets my eyes and slightly bows his head, as if to show he's not planning to go any further.

"No," David bites. He drops his bag and pulls his work shirt over his head. His undershirt is covered in sweat spots and it comes off next to reveal David's hairy chest. He takes his shoes off. I don't care if everyone is looking. I don't care if no one is. David meets my gaze, unbuttons his jeans, and slides them down. I can't help but to rake my eyes down his body. He's muscular in the ways manual labor works the body and thick in the ways that never going to the gym makes him. He's perfect.

Soon, David is in nothing but his boxers. He's giving me the extra seconds I would need to stop him. I don't. He's going to have to take them off and show off that lovely cage of his. I'm practically breathless at his angry strip show. He lets out a whoosh of air, and I can almost hear him ask: *Really? You're going to make me do it?* to which the answer is yes, always yes.

He pulls down his boxers and he looks away from me to glance at the people watching him. Some are, but a naked man isn't exactly unusual here. It means much less to them than it does to him. I bite the key on my necklace and look him up and down.

His eyes narrow onto the key and I can practically hear the thoughts in his head. We haven't been to the Playhouse in a long time. Maybe I brought him here to let him come. I didn't. I drop the key and he follows it as it lands on my breasts.

Alex whistles. "You look fun."

"He is fun," I interrupt, not giving David the agency to answer for himself. "But you'll get to see how much fun he is in a little bit." I hand David the small bag I brought. He is humiliated. He is caged. Yet there is a spark in his eyes that threatens to light me on fire. He can take it. He can take all of this.

"Pick up your clothes, they don't belong on the floor."

He'll have to bend down. He'll have to show his ass to anyone who wants to look.

"Yes, Mistress." He bends over to gather the clothes in his arms. I give him a plastic bag to put them in. He stows it in his backpack.

"I packed some of my toiletries in there. I figured you wouldn't know better and show up a dirty mess."

His jaw clenches, and it feels better than the butterfly kisses he sometimes leaves on my thighs. I'm going to ruin my nice pants if this keeps up for much longer.

"Thank you, Mistress. You think of everything." He doesn't know I have, that these are some of the most feminine smelling brands I could find. He doesn't know that I'll send him back down here after his shower, naked and dripping, smelling like strawberries and lavender rain, flushed with embarrassment. He doesn't know that afterwards, I'll embarrass him even further. He walks away from us to make his way to the shower.

"Your husband is hot. I can't wait to fuck him."

"You aren't allowed to come until I tell you to." I move in front of Alex and open another button on his shirt. He doesn't need it open, but I need my hands on him to gauge him.

"Is that so?" His breathlessness betrays his playful voice.

"I want this to be a slow torture for him. That doesn't happen unless you can keep control of yourself."

"I'll trust you to keep me in check. That way I don't get too crazy with him." He flashes me that same easy smile from before. He's far more confident in his submission than David is. The younger men around here tend to be.

Denial

"Let's make our way upstairs."

The shower upstairs doesn't have a door and we're treated to the sight of David lathering up as we approach. I was hoping the shower would have another couple in it, but he is alone.

"This all smells very flowery, Mistress," David says as we get closer.

"I hope you like it. Oh, don't forget to completely clean yourself up."

David's head snaps up to look at me so fast that water droplets land on my face. *Yes.* His eyes widen as he glances at Alex. He swallows as realization settle on his face. *Gorgeous.* It's not a threesome like he hoped. He's not being cucked like he thought. He's being fucked. He says nothing, and oh my boy is such a good boy.

"I'll see you inside, Alex," I dismiss. Alex backs away but I don't watch him go. I couldn't tear my eyes away from David's face for anything.

"Checking in." This is the first moment I've gotten alone with him since he left for work this morning. He could have stopped this at any time, but he might have felt too pressured to.

"I'm okay." David's voice is strained. He scrubs his body clean. His jaw clenches again and he shakes his head. "Pushed, but okay."

"Good." I won't send him downstairs if he's already feeling pushed. It's only a small mercy, one he won't even appreciate, but I'll save the rest of him for Alex. "Don't use a towel. I'll dry you off in the next room."

He nods silently and rinses my strawberry shampoo out of his hair. "He's such a pretty boy."

"Maybe I like pretty boys," I counter.

He smirks as the suds travel down his body. "He's got no hair for you to pull, and we both know I'm exactly your type."

He's right. He's so right I can't come up with a response. I take a moment to take in the amazing form that David has: strong yet cuddly, intimidating yet soft. I want to step right into that shower with him and kiss all his scars and calluses. I follow a water droplet with my eyes as it travels down his skin, past his belly and his cage.

"Well, maybe there's a reason you're in the cage and he's already in the bedroom." Honey drips like poison off my lips. I grin as his body tenses and I turn to walk away. "Don't forget to clean that ass of yours, so pretty boy can fuck it."

When David arrives in the bedroom, he's got the flush on his face he always has after sticking his fingers up his ass. It's beautiful. I tell him that he's a good boy as I walk up to him with a towel. I pat him dry, kiss him, and then trace some fading marks with my tongue and fingers. He lets out a soft sigh of contentment at the care, and I can't help my grin as I lean in to kiss a fading hickey on his hip.

What if I had a mark that never faded?

"Please tell me it's my turn." Alex practically vibrates with energy. I nod, and Alex bounds over to grab David's face and pull him in for a kiss. David makes a muffled sound of surprise but kisses back. I close the door and then move to my seat and watch in rapt attention.

When I first met this man, he wouldn't even admit when another man was good looking. Now, he's grabbing the ass of the man that's going to fuck him in front of his wife. The growth!

I take off my pants and panties before I ruin them and move the chair to get a better view. Alex pulls back from the kiss and points at the bed. "All fours."

David's head whips around to me. Embarrassed already? His lip twitches. Is he fighting the urge to yell, to buck against the idea of being ordered around like that by someone that isn't me? Is he asking me if I'm really going to make him submit to Alex? I am. I shift, settling into my chair with a grin that says: *yes. Always yes.* His jaw clenches. He closes his eyes. I lick my lips. He's fighting himself, fighting the inevitable.

Without a word, he settles on the bed—on all fours—and looks directly at me. He can be as angry as he wants. He has a choice, and he's choosing to submit.

Alex has full access to him. I have full access to them both.

"What an ass. I can't wait to take it." Alex gives it a light smack, and I think it's only the happy grin on my face that prevents David from decking him.

"Iris brought some lube for me to open you up, but you tell me if it's too much. We'll stop."

"I will." David nods. I make eye contact with Alex above David's head.

"What's your safeword?" I ask David. It's more for Alex than either of us.

"Parachute, or Cracker."

Alex nods, satisfied, and then he grabs David's hips, leans over, and kisses his back. Alex prepares David gently, with encouraging words as he checks in with him, and I'm happy with my choice of a third for the night. It took half a dozen conversations to find him, but he's worth it.

"You are going to take Alex's cock now, David."

David nods and spreads his hands on the bedsheets. He pushes his ass back, taking more of Alex's fingers and Alex pulls out to put a condom on. I lean forward and grab David's chin. He meets my eyes with nervous excitement. I pull his face forward. I start with a light kiss and a gentle nip, and then I deepen the kiss. When David moves, I open my eyes to see Alex grabbing David's hips and lining his cock up. David might want to move his head to watch, but I don't release his jaw.

"Are you sure you want to do this?" Alex asks.

David closes his eyes and inhales. His furrowed brows and tight lips loosen. His lips turn up as he exhales and nods. "I'm sure."

I'm so happy I capture his lips again as Alex starts to push in. Alex lets out a hiss and David groans into my mouth. The bed creaks with the rocking motions of Alex's hips. I pull back and watch as Alex sinks in the last few inches.

Alex leans over David's back. "You smell so good, like a fucking chick."

David accepts the disrespect with an ease that makes me wet. It's all for me. This is all for me. I sit back in my chair and cross my legs. David watches me the entire time that Alex fucks him. I'm tempted to spread my legs and show him what this does to me. I want to run my fingers through my soaking wet pussy and lick my juices up in front of him. Maybe I'd even lean over and reach my hand out so he can taste me. I squeeze my legs shut and watch.

"This is torture." David chokes on a low moan. Alex is pounding a steady rhythm that must be setting off fireworks behind his eyes. If I angle my head the right way, I can watch his caged cock sway.

"I know." I slowly smile as he looks at me. "This brings me so much joy. I can't begin to tell you how much."

Eventually, David surrenders. "Please give me a break, Mistress."

Alex shifts his hands on David's back but continues to fuck him slowly. Does Alex's cock burn David's insides in a way my toys don't? Is it easier or harder for him to be fucked by flesh? Does he have a preference? I can't watch his face when I fuck him unless it's in a mirror, but in this position I can see every shudder and hear every small moan. I can watch him clench the sheets and let out small hisses as Alex goes deeper.

Denial

"No." I open my legs to show him my bare pussy. Does it glisten for him in this light? He has to be able to tell how wet I am either way. He can probably smell it. David groans and his eyes blow out in hunger. Alex stops for a second, looks over to my pussy, and then fucks David even harder.

"Fuck!" Alex groans, and I'm not sure if David is clenching around him or if it's from the sight of me. It makes me want more either way.

"I'll tell you what," I say to David. "If you let him come in you, just like this, I'll plug you and let you eat me out."

"You will?"

"I will. Now beg the nice man to continue to fuck you. It was incredibly rude of you to suggest he stop."

Alex grins as David lets out a whimper. After a few incredibly long seconds, David asks Alex to continue. I frown and David furrows his brows. He swallows and then he closes his eyes as he begins to beg. He begs for forgiveness. He begs to be fucked. He begs Alex to come in his ass.

Alex curses and begins to fuck David harder. "I'm going to fill you up so good."

"Please."

"I'm going to fuck you so hard you can't walk." Alex changes his pattern to fast hard thrusts that make the bed protest angrily.

"Fuck you, pretty boy."

"I think you're pretty too," Alex groans. He lets out a string of curses before uttering the perfect words to fuck with David. "Please, can I come?" Alex asks, balls deep in my husband. I grin.

My husband practically growls. "What?"

"Oh Alex, you'll have to ask better than that." I cross my legs. My husband growls again and Alex covers David's mouth with his hand. Alex begs, and I swear I can taste David's anger in the air.

"Alex," I make sure to clarify, "you can come."

"Thank you." Alex's eyes are hot as he meets mine. He lets out a series of small groans as he comes, and David lets out a string of curses.

Alex murmurs something to David, kissing his shoulder and laughing softly. He stands and pulls out of David slowly, and David grunts at the change. I move forward to wipe the sweat off David's head with a towel. "Are you okay?"

His jaw clenches but he nods.

Alex grabs his clothes. "I had a lot of fun." He places a knee on the bed and kisses David again. David looks a bit calmer now, and even admits that he had fun as well. I'll be able to coax more out of him after Alex leaves. It's a quiet, but not awkward, moment as Alex dresses himself.

"I'd love to join you again." Alex straightens his shirt and pants. As I smooth down David's hair, Alex rolls his sleeves up and pops his collar. I walk him to the door and he gives me a kiss on the cheek and a hug goodbye.

"I'll message you and see if we can't set something else up," I say. "You were great today."

"Bye!" He waves to David and then leaves, closing the door behind him. I turn to David, but before I can say anything he lifts me from my spot by the door and tosses me on the bed. He lays on me with his head in my stomach and he trembles. His warm hands crawl under my shirt as his breath tickles the hair on my belly button.

"Please tell me. I'm begging you. Add another day, add another ten days, but please give me an end date."

"No."

"I hate this." His fingers tighten around my hips. Then he dives for my pussy with such fervor all I can do is moan in response.

"I promised to plug you." My protests are weak.

"Then tell me to stop." He growls into my pussy, sucking on my clit and forcing my thighs apart.

I don't.

7 – Pressure

The last accessory for our lunch date is in our little toy chest. The second I open it, David appears over my shoulder. His hands wrap around my waist as he kisses my neck. The slow and teasing kisses are full of promises and temptation. I lean back into his warmth with a soft sigh, and he tightens his grip as his kisses grow longer and hotter. Finally, I twist my head, give him a quick kiss, and pull away from him to get back to my box. The chain is in here somewhere.

He follows. He trails his warm hands down to my hips and leans in close enough that his stubble scratches my neck. "What are we doing today, love?" He's been asking every day since I put a heart sticker on the calendar in today's slot. I've been building the day up with sly comments but I haven't told him anything direct.

"You'll see soon enough." I push aside the ropes and cuffs and the bag of dildos. It's not under the lube packets or the butt plugs. David peppers soft kisses across my shoulders as I rummage through the bin. I close my eyes with a gasp as he bites my neck and moves his hand under my waistband. My nipples harden as goosebumps race up my arms.

The moan slips out of me before I can stop it. At this rate we won't make the lunch reservation. "Behave."

His hand slowly retreats, teasing the skin above my waistband. He continues to nibble on my skin, electrifying me. "But I can be such a *good* boy for you," he murmurs.

He could, but then we'd be late for lunch. My hands finally wrap around the cold links, and I pull them out as I turn in his arms. His smirk falls as he looks at the nipple clamps in my hand. It's not his favorite toy, and I'm sure he'd rather kneel and have an early lunch than wear them, but he'll do anything at this point. That's how desperate he is to come.

"If you wear the nipple clamps in public today while we go eat lunch, I'll suck your cock until you want me to stop." I shake the chains in front of him. They jingle and his pupils blow out as he swallows. He locks eyes with me. Have they always been so dark and rich in their brownness?

He looks at the clamps but doesn't answer right away. This was a spur of the moment purchase we haven't used in years. We've done this before and enjoyed it in short bursts. We haven't done it while he was caged. We haven't done this in public. We haven't done this for that long. His gaze shifts from the clamps to me, and the raw desire and hunger in his eyes steals my breath from me. He's going to agree. Has he always looked at me like he never wanted to see anything else?

"You will?" His voice sounds like it's scraping on gravel, low and rough.

"I will," I promise. I'll lick and suck his cock. I'll pull his foreskin back and swirl my tongue in circles around his head. I'll pump my hand up and down his shaft slowly as I kiss the tip of his cock and I'll play with his balls and bob on his cock until he wants me to stop. I'll do all of it, but I won't let him come.

"I'll do it. Of course, I'll do it. As it pleases you, Mistress."

I grin. David doesn't know. I don't tell him. Why would I? The thrill of my white lie causes the blood pumping in my heart to echo in my clit and my breath to catch. Of course, sucking his cock doesn't mean letting him come. He'll learn. Oh, he'll learn at the worst moment. My lips fall open. He'd still do it, likely. Knowing before he does is just a bonus. With him, this lopsided deal is something I never have to apologize for.

I pinch the clasps in my finger, opening and closing them with a feral grin. Can he see it on my face? Does he know why? Can he guess? Is it better if he knows now? No. I want to see his hope break after he's built it up over lunch. His brow will furrow before his whole face falls in realization. Will he cry?

I break eye contact to kiss him, and it's like a cord of tension snaps in the way he wraps his arms around me and kisses me. I'm 18 again, I'm 28, I'm 38. I'm young and desperate and scrambling for this man like I'll die if I don't have him. I'm sneaking out of windows and giggling as we drunkenly stumble home. I'm swaying at our first dance. We're shoving pieces of cake in each other's mouths.

If we keep going like this, we won't even make it to lunch. I pull back but he leans down, kissing my neck as he follows me. His beard drags on my skin, and goosebumps rise up to meet him. I press a hand to his chest to push him back and he locks eyes with me again. He's flushed and grinning. My face is warm. I'm probably flushed too. He pulls his shirt off and looks down at my little chain. I'm practically panting as I lift it.

"Someone's excited," David mumbles as I attach the first one to his left nipple.

I lower the little metal ring along the tweezers to make it snug but not terribly tight. I'm going for longevity here. "I am." I won't tell him why. My secret is like a vibe between my legs, thrumming over me with wave after wave of excitement. Once the second clamp is on, I step back. "You'll probably need your jacket for lunch now."

"This is going to be torture."

"I hope so." I tug slightly on the chain.

David closes his eyes and lets out a small wince. "Alright. Does that mean it's time to go?"

I drive us there, tugging on his chain at every red light and stop sign. He pants in the car, reclines his seat, and groans as I tease him. I glance at his jeans but he's caged and won't be sporting any erections any time soon. Only the flush on his face gives us away.

"How are you doing?" I ask as we pull into the parking lot.

"I can't wait for you to suck my cock," David groans. I give him a long tug. I can't wait for it either. The look on his face when he realizes he doesn't get to come is going to be priceless.

His flush stays on his face, dark and deep, as we enter the restaurant and sit next to each other at a booth. Is he embarrassed? Do people think he's nervous? He looks over the menu, and I use the shield to tug on the chain of the clamps once more. He stiffens in his seat but is silent. Good boy. I pull on the chain to provide tension, and I release it to give him relief. His flush never leaves his face. Maybe the waiter will think it's a sunburn. I don't care what the waiter thinks, I'm going to make the most of the clamps before the food comes out.

When the waiter arrives, David orders stiffly, voice straining as he fights to keep his composure. The cage must help with that. His poor cock must be throbbing and pulsing, begging to be let out. Once it's out, I'm going to make it worse for him. It'll be swollen and thick, a bead of precum sitting on the tip as he pants and fists the bed sheets. I lick my lips, and David bites his as he stares. Does he know what I'm thinking about? I place my order next, but the only thing I want in my mouth right now is him. I'll pull his foreskin back and lick the rim of his head to start. It might not even take that to make him beg. He might start as soon as I take his cage off. I tug slightly on the chain when the waiter walks away. It's a shame he can't wear this all day. He'll probably need them off once we get to the car, but his nipples will still be sore and ripe for teasing. He might scream when I finally wrap my lips around them and suck.

"What are you thinking about?" David rasps.

"The same thing you are." I tug on the clamps harder and he leans forward as his mouth opens in a tiny, barely audible gasp. "I'm wondering how long it'll take until you beg."

"I could beg now, if you want." He groans softly. Does the table next to us hear? What would they think? What would happen if David slid to his knees in front of everyone?

"Right here, you'd beg, properly?"

"Maybe." He's not looking around at anyone else. He's looking at me with an unmistakable heat in his eyes. Maybe he would slide right off the chair and go to his knees in the middle of the restaurant. Maybe he doesn't care that we'd get kicked out and someone he knows may see.

My pussy throbs, clenching on nothing. Fuck, I'm soaking wet. I release the chain to grab his hand and guide it to my open legs beneath the table. His eyes narrow and his pupils blow as he cups me. I close my eyes and lean back as he slowly rubs his palm against my clit, back and forth, like he can't believe it. David presses down and my eyes shoot open as pleasure alights my entire body. We're in public, but I can't tell him to stop, not when I already feel close. I lean my head on his shoulders, spread my legs further, and pray that the longer tablecloth hides us.

"David," I murmur into his shoulder. He inhales sharply and his hand presses against me firmly. I grind my hips into him. Electricity dances across my skin, lighting me on fire. Fuck the tablecloth, I don't care who sees anymore. I need him closer, I need him in me. I need to clench around his cock and scream.

"You're fucking sexy. Will you come for me, just like this?" His stubble drags on my cheek as he growls in my ear. Does it look obvious, or like he's giving me a kiss as we cuddle on a date?

I might scream for him, just like this. My face warms but I refuse to pant. "I might," I admit. "I might soon."

David turns away from me, lifting his water to drink as he rubs faster with his other hand. It's maddening. It's sexy. He moves my panties aside and slides a finger into my pussy. I grab the edge of the table as my eyes widen, but no one is looking. He slides a second finger in. The angle makes it impossible for him to get deep, and the tease is driving me crazy. My hips grind down hard, searching for more. Instead of giving me more, he rubs my clit with his palm, slow and steady, as his fingers continue their shallow thrusts. Everything is slow, but my heart is racing. Everything is quiet, but my ears ring. Heat settles low in my stomach and I hold back a moan as David slowly, perfectly, works my pussy into overdrive. The low buzz of conversation and the music playing from the speakers may be enough to hide the sound of his fingers in my pussy, but it's not enough to hide my moan. I bite my tongue and clench my fist to stay quiet.

David's not even fazed. The bastard. How can keep sipping his water as if he's not finger fucking me? I tug on his chain. He retaliates by pressing down on my clit hard enough that I curl forward. One of us kicks the table, and the glass rattles, but it feels so good that I don't care if anyone hears us. I don't care if we get kicked out. I want his tongue on my clit and his cock in me. I want to come again and again on his cock as I scream. My orgasm builds and builds in silence until I can't take it anymore. I turn and bite his shoulder and he pumps me all through my silent orgasm. I blink hard after the waves of pleasure subside, and I'm panting softly as he retreats, sliding my ruined panties back into place.

My orgasm does the opposite of sate me. I want more, more, *more*.

The waiter sets our food on the table in front of us. My heart beat drums in my ears and I can't make out whatever the waiter says as he departs. I have no clue if the pasta in front of me is even what I ordered. David nudges my leg as he gestures to the food.

The *bastard.*

My face burns as he lifts a bite of fettuccini into his mouth. His lips twitch into a smirk as he meets my eyes. "Aren't you hungry, dear?" He licks the fork and hums. That tongue should be on my clit right now, should be pressing against my folds and licking my cream, not the damned alfredo sauce. "Finger licking good." He closes his eyes and darts his tongue out to slip between his middle and pointer finger as he licks himself clean of me.

I do the only logical thing I can: grab the chain connected to his nipple clamps and *pull*. The clips make a small click as they release his nipples and David's fist meets the table as he groans. His fork clatters down. I clench the chains in my hand and force out a laugh. "That good?" I stab my fork into his fettucine and come away with a small piece of chicken. I can't even taste it.

"How are we doing on those first couple bites?" The waiter's eyes are tired, but they aren't suspicious.

I wave my fork around. "Fantastic, isn't it, honey?"

David's hand lands on my thigh as he smiles at the waiter. "Wonderful." His fingers squeeze so tightly my thigh jerks. He holds it in place and clenches tight enough that pressure tips into pain and I grab his wrist as the waiter leaves.

"David."

His fingers tighten but his voice is level. "I can't believe you just did that."

I slap his hand, and he releases me at once. His fingers leave pink circles on my thigh as he reaches for his fork and shoves pasta in his mouth. I find my voice a second later. "Too much?"

"No," David growls, meeting my eyes. My pussy clenches as my mouth dries. Oh wow. He's hungry, but nothing in this restaurant is going to satisfy him. His tongue licks the corner of his mouth as his eyes drop to my lips. He inhales deeply, nostrils flaring, as his gaze drops lower. His exhale rumbles through his chest like he's some kind of animal.

Lunch is a blur.

The drive home is a blur.

Everything is a blur until I get David back home and naked and in my mouth. He bucks as I suck on his nipples, whimpers as I unlock his cage, and screams out when I take him into my mouth with a long and hard suck. He hardens instantly. He gently threads his fingers in my hair as I give him long licks and soft sucks. I cup his neglected balls as I pull his foreskin back.

"Fuck, finally."

I suck on the head of his cock, swirling my tongue around the ridges of his head, and his hands tighten in my hair. He sighs out in pleasure as I pump his shaft slowly with my hand. He murmurs words I can't make out, pushing me down to take more of him in my mouth. I let him. I bob on his cock and play with his balls as he bucks into me.

I focus my attention on the head of his cock, and he smooths the hair away from my face.

"So good to me…" he mutters. "I love the way you suck my cock."

He won't love it when I stop. I suck harder and squeeze my hands. His hips buck reflexively. I pepper sloppy kisses up and down his shaft and then take the head into my mouth again.

"It feels so good." David's hand tightens around my hair. His hips lift off the bed. His cock swells in my mouth. His murmurs cut off.

I pull back, letting him fall out. His cock bobs and the temptation to bring him back into my mouth makes me bite my lips. He's too close to chance it.

"Are you going to make me beg?" he sighs out. Silence. "Iris?" His voice breaks on my name. I don't think I've heard anything that beautiful before.

"I said I would suck your cock, not that I would let you come," I remind him as I sit up. His cock practically bounces as David clenches his whole body. I stifle a laugh.

"You said as long as I want." His voice picks up a dangerous edge.

My smile turns feral. "I'll go as long as you want. That doesn't mean you get to come today."

His cock twitches again, but David lets out a sigh and sinks into the bed. "Okay." Defeat coats the word, and it tastes so very sweet. "Okay."

"Did you really think you would?" I rub salt in his wounds.

He swallows and covers his face with his hand. "Of course, I did. You wanted me to think I would."

I did.

"Yes."

He lets out a sigh and then grabs the headboard with both of his hands. "Edging?"

"Of course. Unless you want me to stop now?"

"No." He surrenders. He doesn't want to. His hands and jaw clench, but he surrenders. I need to take in every detail of it. The harsh rise and fall of his chest. The angry vein on his forehead. I trace the lines of his muscles as his fingers clench the headboard. They turn white before he releases his grip.

By the time I return my attention to his poor cock, it's sagging and leaking. It looks as defeated as David does. I grab him and squeeze, but he doesn't make a sound. He doesn't protest the edging. He doesn't ask to come, even as he grows harder in my hand. I take his head into my mouth and suck away the drops of precum. He softens and I open my eyes to stare at him and he's…

He's crying.

His eyes are closed. His hands grip the headboard tight enough that his forearms bulge. His mouth moves without sound. Tears steadily fall from his eyes to roll down his cheeks. I'd hoped he'd cry, but this isn't as satisfying as I'd expected.

"David?" I release his cock. He shakes his head.

"Are you okay?" I try again.

"This is what you want," he grits out. "Take it. Unless you're going to let me come, which I *know* you're not, then please don't ask me anything." His arms tremble with the force of his clenched hands. "Just use me and then put me back in the cage, please."

"David…" I trail off. How can I get him excited for this?

"I want to serve you, so please just use me."

"David, I—"

"Use me," he demands.

It's fire in my veins. He hates this. He hates all of this but he'll do it for me. Fuck. When we got married, his vows included a promise to serve me. He'd said '*This I promise you. I will be your servant; both when it is easy and when it is hard*'. I haven't thought of those vows in what feels like forever. My smile isn't sadistic this time, but soft. I'm certainly making it hard now, and look at him.

I touch his cock and he breaks. I lightly stroke him as my heart beats to the rhythm of his sobs and my eyes find every tear that falls for me. Until, finally, he shakes his head. "You can stop now."

We're reaching the end soon, but we're not there yet.

<u>8 – Hate</u>

My sundress is loose. I'm wearing panties I don't care about. David is taking a break from the cage to prevent chafing, and my parents are still thirty minutes away. I set the alarm on my phone for ten minutes and call David into the room.

I twist the phone to show the timer. "My parents will be here in ten minutes. If you can give me three orgasms in that time, I'll let you come." I hit start.

"That's impossible, Mistress." He unbuckles his pants and kicks them off. He's hard already, leaking at the tip and so full it's almost purple in color. I lick my lips. He pulls his shirt off and crosses the room in long quick strides.

I smirk. "Then you better get started."

He growls in a primal way as he snatches my phone and tosses it onto the bed. Before I can react, he lifts me onto the bed and rips my panties as he pulls them to the side. He pushes my head down into the bed without grace, and I flail.

"David!" I exclaim, shocked and turned on. He shoves my dress over my hips as he lines his hot cock up with my wet pussy.

He slides in slowly, but that's where his restraint ends. Once he is settled in fully and knows he won't hurt me, his fingers tighten around my hips and he begins fucking me at a brutal pace. I push against the bed to get onto all fours, but he pushes my shoulders down—pushes my face into the bed—to expose me further to him.

"David—" The scold turns into a moan halfway through as his cock lights my insides on fire. He's never been this rough with me before, but I already love it. His hands tighten on my hips until it tips the line into pain and I groan. Maybe ten minutes was too much time. My breaths turn into pants. Too much. Not enough. I repeat his name as I try to push up but all I can do is grip the bed sheets.

I push my hips backwards into him as I feel my orgasm approaching. A thousand stars burst behind my eyelids as he slams into me.

It's fast. It's good. The bed squeaks its protests as he somehow goes faster, or deeper, or harder. I can't tell anymore. All I know is that I need it. I need more. The tight vice grip David has on my hips keeps me from moving away, even as his thrusts get harder, almost to the point of pain. The delicious little stretch that enhances the feeling.

"Fuck!" My pussy walls clench around him. I'm close. *I'm close.* A little more.

"There we go," he encourages.

My first orgasm washes over me seconds later and I yell into the bed sheets as my world explodes. He slows his thrusts slightly as I come down from it. He moves his hands to rub my back and I let out a softer, longer, moan. "Those were my favorite panties," I say a few seconds later, once I can breathe again.

"I don't care." His thrusts become brutal once more, sliding in and out of my pussy with ease. It's like he's even faster now. Sensation dances everywhere and I can't focus. I can't even muster the energy to be mad at his comment because I love what his anger is doing to the way he's fucking me.

I'd stop wearing panties for good if sex was always like this. I'd keep him in that cage forever. His cock feels impossibly hot, impossibly hard, like if he thrusted in the right way, he'd tear me in two and I'd die in blissful agony. My soaking wet pussy makes an embarrassing sound as his hips slap against my ass. David grunts, but he is a man on a mission, and doesn't stop.

"Yes, *yes!*" I can't stop talking, praising, moaning. My whole body tightens slowly, my toes, my fingers, my legs. *Yes.* My thighs and my pussy quiver. How much time is left? I can't lift my head to look.

"Two," he mutters, growls, pants? I'm not sure. I only know he's right in claiming my second orgasm as I scream into the mattress. He slows again slightly and I'm not sure if it's on purpose or because I'm clenching him too tight. My hips stutter. Wetness gushes between my legs and the only sounds I can make are all needy moans and pants.

How much time is left?

Seconds later, David picks up his pace, like a machine. I already feel close to the edge. I clench my hands into the bedsheets and try to hold on. I cry out as arousal throbs throughout my whole body. I'm falling and *falling* and I'm close but I can't.

"Stop holding back." His whisper is harsh.

I bite the bedsheets to muffle my scream, but it doesn't work. "I'm not holding back."

"I can feel you holding back. Give me your orgasm," David demands.

"You're going to have to take it." My words are cocky, but the reality is that my pussy is pulsing and desperate. I take slow measured breaths. I need to hold on. My moans fill the room but I can't let him win. I'm not done yet.

He changes tactics, slowing his thrusts and reaching a hand between my legs to work a finger along my clit. My legs are embarrassingly chilly as he nudges them apart. I sob. I'm close. I'm close. I'm oh so close. It wouldn't be that bad to end the game early would it? We can always play again. If he deserves it, I should—should—

The alarm goes off.

Saved by the bell, literally. David freezes behind me in realization, but I can do nothing but breathe. I'm too close, I can barely think straight. He's waiting for me to speak something, obviously, but all I can do is take slow measured breaths into the mattress and try not to laugh. His orgasm denial has gotten deep enough I have to deny my own orgasm. What monster did I unleash? How do I do it again? I slowly push myself onto all fours.

"That was only two."

Denial

He crumbles behind me. "I can't." His hands loosen around my hips, but his cock twitches inside me. "Please don't make me stop."

I turn my head. The sight of his tears is better than a third orgasm, with the way my whole body tingles at the sight of it. My pussy walls clench around his cock.

David whimpers, "Please. You already own me; you don't have to prove it this way."

I own him in the way of collars and leashes, in the way of rings and marriage, but this is a new level of ownership, and I'm drunk off of the power. "You should get dressed."

"I hate you," he growls as he rips himself away from me. I'm sure he believes it. I'm empty at his departure, and I turn on the bed to watch him pant. *I* believe it. Still, he doesn't make a move for his cock, doesn't give it the few strokes that would bring him over the edge. Just for me. It's all for me. He snatches the cage off of the toy chest and storms out of the bedroom.

I don't think I've ever loved him as much as I do right now.

9 – Love

Something about David when he's sleeping is so… fragile.

It's not pretty. Drool stains his cheek, and his mouth is open at an odd angle, but something about it draws me in all the same. It's not even peaceful. He snores like he's boasting to the world that he's able to sleep anywhere at any time, but the hard lines of his face have softened into something vulnerable.

Washed in the dim lights of the city outside, he looks breakable in a way he doesn't during the day. Maybe it's that he can't see me or stop me from doing whatever I want. He can't see the intent behind my eyes or hear the danger in my voice. He's here, mine for the taking. It sharpens me into something predatory.

David didn't stir when I escaped from our bed, didn't even shift as I shoved him off of me. If he hasn't already woken up, the list of what I can do to him before he does is exceedingly long. The list of things he's given me permission to do is virtually endless.

I twist the scissors in my hand, pressing the sharp tip into my palm just enough that I let out a deep breath at the sensation.

My nipples harden as I tug the blanket off, revealing him to me. His belly shakes with his snores, rising and falling as his legs twitch. Are they cold? Maybe his dream changed from something pleasant to unpleasant. Maybe he can subconsciously sense the danger. His boxers are bunched at the spot where his leg meets his groin, and the silver rings gleam. Righteousness settles in my core. He belongs caged up in my bed, mine for the taking.

He doesn't care for these boxers, and there's a hole in the side. I cut them off without remorse. The cage is warm and heavy. I cup his delicate balls in my hand; they're heavier than I remember. How long has it been now, since he's felt the relief of coming? Does he remember how? He's been such a good boy. Does that make me the big bad wolf?

I spread my fingers out against his thigh. It's beautiful and unmarred and it should be mine. Oh, if only I could bite him hard enough to draw blood right now, but that would certainly wake him up.

Maybe when he wakes up…

If I bit him hard enough to scar, then he'd be marked even in the dark. I'd be able to blindly feel for it, and know he always has my mark on him. He shifts, opening his thigh up to me, and I jerk my hand back.

He wants more than a bite mark.

I push against his bare hip, pulling the boxers away as he rolls over. He grunts in his sleep, and shifts into his new position without waking. His ass is covered in bruises but I can barely make them out in the dark. I'd be able to make out a brand in the dark, wouldn't I? Instead of revulsion, excitement fills me at the thought. I swallow the thought as I palm his ass then swap the scissors for the bottle of lube as I grab my harness.

The lube is cold, and I let it warm up before circling the rim of his asshole with my finger. He doesn't stir, but I didn't think he would. He's snoring loud enough to drown out the world outside. He still feels safe enough to sleep. I slide a finger into his ass with a grin. He's never safe from me. Awake. Asleep. He'd never deny me anything.

Denial

More lube, more fingers. He's dead to the world. There's no rush, no one to interrupt me. I slowly spread him wide open. Resistance gives way to softness. He shifts again, sliding his leg down, but I stop him with my other hand. I need him to stay nice and open for me.

The double penetration harness has a bigger and smaller side. Both of them vibrate. The bigger side is mine. I tighten the straps around my waist and line up the silicone tip to my pussy.

Have I been this wet the whole time?

I slide my part of the dildo in with ease and a small gasp. It's bigger than David, longer, wider, and firmer. I roll my hips into it, fucking myself with a few quick thrusts. He's clueless, still snoring face down and ripe for the taking. He said he likes that I can fuck him with my cock and come over and over again while he has no idea. Usually when he wakes, he gets to come too, but will he like it if he wakes and can't?

I line up his end with his asshole and pour a generous amount of lube on it. He won't wake up. I could slap his ass and he wouldn't wake. I could do almost anything and he wouldn't wake. I slide the head of my cock past his rim slowly, and the other end shifts inside of me, pressing the tiniest bit deeper.

There's no need to hide my groan. I roll my hips, pulling his hips towards me as the silicone hits all the right spots. "Fuck."

I roll my hips again, starting a slow and steady pace that warms my insides. Heat settles everywhere as I get bolder, pulling his hips to meet mine. He's still fucking snoring! What's he dreaming about? Each thrust is a little faster, a little deeper, than the last. Will he be sad to know he missed this while he was dreaming? Maybe he'll feel violated, despite what he'd said before. I gasp as waves of pleasure shoot from my core all the way to my toes. Is his poor little cock leaking? He'll wake up wet on both sides and have no idea what I've done to him.

I grunt, and shift my hips, and the entire bed shifts with me.

My jaw falls open. My hips stutter with the desire to bite him—to draw blood and mark him and keep him. Instead, I bite my lip hard enough that copper fills my mouth. He can't see my face. He can't read into anything I say. It gives the thought freedom to grow.

What would be so bad about branding him?

I let the fantasy take me away as I thrust into him. The slick sounds of my cock in David's ass can't rival his snores, but I try. I fuck him harder and louder. I pull on his hip, digging my fingers into his soft skin. He stops mid-snore and grunts in disorientation. I press on his back and slam into him harder.

"What?" Confusion coats his word as much as sleepiness does.

I don't answer him. Why would I? I'm already getting what I want and he won't stop me. I groan into his back, and now that he's not snoring, every movement and sound is obnoxiously loud. His hand fists in the sheets, but I pull on his elbow to prevent him from getting any leverage.

"Iris?" There's no fear, only confusion in his voice.

I thrust into him harder, and his hips jerk into me as he groans.

"Fuck," he groans into the pillow. When he fists it again, I let him. He isn't going to fight me now.

"Finally awake?" I lean over and finally sink my teeth into his back.

He bucks. "Iris!"

"That's right," I growl into his skin. "What was I supposed to do when you leave yourself so open and vulnerable to me?"

"G—God!" He shudders as I reach forward to feel his cock straining to grow erect against its cage. I shift my hips to fuck his prostate and grunt in approval as he gasps at the sudden sensation.

I fuck him harder and faster, as the buzz of my orgasm hums in the back of my head. "So helpless. Did you feel safe in your sleep? Do you have any idea the wicked things I want to do to you?"

"Mistress!" He begins to sob. "I'm so tight in the cage!"

Fire ignites in my veins. Heat settles in my core. "Oh, you poor baby. You didn't think this was for you, did you?"

He shifts, trying to get up on all fours. Maybe it's to help me, maybe it's to get away. "Ple—"

"No." I press against him with all my weight. "You stay there and you take this. Take everything."

"Please let me out, please let me out," he begs. "Fuck, this feels so—please let me come, Mistress, please. I can't—"

"You will."

His begging is enough to send me over the edge. "I can't—"

"You will." I fist my hand in his hair and shove it into the bed. Yes. *Yes!* Whatever he mumbles into the pillow is lost to my scream. Wave after wave of pleasure wash over me as my hips stutter against his. My muscles spasm and my throat throbs. Stars dance in my vision as I clench around the hard silicone of the toy. I wish I could fill his ass with it so he'd remember what happened as it leaked out. The lube will have to do.

He turns his head to look at me, but I can't read him.

Is he horny? Is he disgusted? I wipe the sweat off my brow as I pull out of him. He lets out a sigh. Lube leaks out of his ass and my pussy clenches again. I close my eyes against the pleasure and unbuckle the harness. He twists one way, then the other, cracking his back.

"That was—wow. You're planning to kill me, aren't you?"

I meet his eyes. It's too dark to make them out. I pull the dildo out and whimper at the loss. Fuck the mess, I can't be this far away from him when I can't make out his eyes. I drop the harness and crawl over to him on the bed. I run my hands up and down his back. He's shaking.

"You love me right?" Desperation laces his words. "This is because you love me, right?"

"I cannot begin to tell you how much I love you." I kiss him everywhere I can touch, careful to be tender, not erotic. "All of this makes me love you more."

He sits up and kisses me. It's sweet and soft and my eyes warm. He cups my face in his hand. "I just want to make you happy."

"I'm proud of you," I blurt, putting my hand on his chest.

His lips turn up, but his sexual frustration is clear. "Thank you."

"There is a woman being proposed to right now, another one is having her first child, and there is a woman giving an acceptance speech. And yet, with all that, I can tell you I'm the happiest woman alive right now."

He closes his eyes, dislodging tears. They disappear in the darkness as they fall to the bed. "I love you so much."

My heart swells. "I know." If I had been anything less than his everything, this would be over by now. It would have been over a very long time ago.

I bring a warm towel to the bedroom and gently wipe away the mess I've made of him. Once he stops crying and gets cleaned up, almost all the evidence of my moonlight transformation vanishes. I guide him to the shower to wash away the rest.

Once David turns the shower on, and I've cleaned the bedroom, I stare at a familiar contact on my phone and try to calm my racing heart.

I hit the call button and lift the phone to my ear before I can back out. I turn David's key over in my hand.

"Hello, my dear." Thorn's warm and friendly tone somehow sends goosebumps up my arms. Can I really do this? "I'm locking up the Playhouse. How are you?"

I just had some of the best sex of my life and now I'm in a panic. What else can I say? "I'm good."

"What can I do for you?"

"Do you have time this week for me to stop by the shop?" My voice shakes, but Thorn doesn't point it out.

"Is this what I think it's about? I told David not to give up on the idea." I can practically see the teasing smile spreading across his face as he fiddles with something. His hands are always busy.

David already talked to him about this? I'm too far from my comfort zone now to be ribbed about it. "Thorn." What should have been a scold sounds like a plea, and he laughs. My heart has somehow crawled its way into my throat and I drag my finger along the key's ridges as I stare at the bathroom door. David has given me everything. He's *giving* me everything. Maybe I can give him this.

"Talk to me about branding."

10 – <u>Unlocked</u>

The key to David's cock cage is on the counter.

I hang my bag by the front door and pause at the sight. It's his key. He's retrieved his emergency key from the bathroom and now it's on the counter. David stands right next to it, staring at it. He doesn't look hurt. He didn't message me anything about needing it off for safety. His eyes are red from crying. Shame colors his face as well and he can't even look at me. He's not wearing his collar either.

Is he quitting?

He jerks at the sound of the door closing behind me. "I'm sorry."

"For what?"

109

He's in sweats. I can't immediately tell if the cage is on right now. I can't tell if he's this ashamed because he's contemplating ending early or if it's guilt for already ending early. I slowly walk towards him. His cage isn't on the table or the counter.

I don't reach for the key.

"I couldn't think about anything else today after our morning edging, after *last night*. I called off work. I was furious, and then I cried, and then I…" He gestures to the key on the table. "I was hating you," he confesses, "and I was blaming the cage and I unlocked it."

He unlocked it without me, he means. He'd been out of the cage many times since we started, but I've always been there. It's always been my key. "Did you take it off?"

He shakes his head. "I couldn't." He falls to his knees in front of me and wraps his arms around my legs. "I'm so sorry. I couldn't do it. You weren't here. I broke your trust."

Look at this man. Look at what this man is doing for me. I'm the luckiest woman in the world.

"What do you want to happen now?" What do *I* want to happen now? He's trembling against my legs. He had to call off of work. I can't do this to him forever. I need to end this.

"Please lock me back up," he begs. "Take both keys."

"I can't take both keys. What if something happens?"

"Please!" He's crying. Surprisingly, a wave of arousal climbs up from my toes to my core. I'm wet at the sight. My skin erupts into goosebumps and my nipples harden against my bra. I want to make him cry more. "I can't go on if the temptation is right there. I'm weak." He's so strong. So beautiful. "Punish me, please. I'm so sorry."

"Get the cane and get undressed."

He scampers away from me to grab my cane. I only look back at the counter once he's left the room. The key shines on it, mocking me. It's small and silver with a round top, yet it feels bigger. It holds too much power. Its very presence today has tipped the scales. I'm still staring at it when David comes back into the room, holding my cane.

He's still wearing the locked cage.

He kneels to offer me the cane as he looks down at the ground. I take it from him without a sound, and he waits for another command. I turn the cane over in my hand. Do I want to punish him? No. He hasn't actually done anything wrong. Will he be racked with guilt and ruin the game if I don't punish him? Can I convince him that he hasn't done wrong? The whole reason he has the key is if he needs it. It's the equivalent of a physical safeword. I would never—could never—punish him for safewording. I won't punish him for considering it.

He won't be satisfied unless I hurt him, though. I turn the cane over again in my hands. His hands reach for me, and tug on my pants to pull me a step closer. He presses his head into my thighs. I run my fingers through his hair. His tears leave damp spots against my pants. There is no way he'd believe he didn't do anything wrong when he's like this. I'll have to hit him. His hands tug down as he sinks into a sitting position, but he doesn't release my legs.

"Stay." I slowly step out of his embrace. He lowers his hands to lay by his knees. He doesn't look up. I squeeze his shoulder before moving away from him then I tear off my work clothes and get into comfortable pajamas. He is sitting in the same spot when I return. I direct him to stand in the center of the living room, where I have him pull down the cuffs hanging from the ropes on the ceiling. I run my fingers over the calluses on his palm as I take his hand into mine.

I have to try. "You didn't do anything wrong."

"I'm sorry."

"You didn't do anything wrong," I repeat as I lace our fingers together. He doesn't believe me. He won't look at me. I push his chin up with my hand and then lean in to give him a soft kiss. His lips are soft and pliant against my own, but he kisses me slowly and reflexively. He doesn't press against me or seek more from my kiss. I press against him harder, but he keeps the kiss soft. "Do you want to talk about this? Why did you want to stop?"

He shakes his head and looks down. Where is the guilt stemming from? Did he actually take the cage all the way off, holding it in these very hands? Did regret set in with the click of the lock or once he sprung free? Or is the regret more than today? Does he wish we never started? I grab the cuff dangling next to me and cuff his wrist. He lifts his other hand in offering and I cuff it as well. I push on his shoulders until he kneels. The cuffs don't have much slack and his arms are pulled above his head as he drops to his knees. His hands hang limp instead of grabbing the ropes and I frown at them.

"What's wrong?" I ask. He doesn't answer. "David, say something."

"I'm sorry."

"Say something else."

"Green."

I purse my lips. He doesn't say anything as I cross my arms in front of him. He gets like this sometimes—stuck in his own head. He won't say anything until I break down the wall he's built up, literally pulling it out of him with pain. If he wants to be difficult, I can beat it out of him. I gently tap the cane against his back, gauging his reaction. He's silent.

"I'm not going to punish you." I press the cane into his back. He doesn't respond. I huff as I increase the strength of each strike, gradually going up in force and frequency. Finally, I pause. "Say something."

"Green."

He lets out a hiss as the cane bounces off of his skin.

It's not a punishment.

He must know. Nothing about this matches our punishment routine. We haven't gone over the broken rule. We didn't agree to a punishment. We haven't agreed to a correction. So, I don't make him count and he doesn't say anything to stop me.

He must know that this isn't a punishment.

The next impact echoes in the room, and I loosen my hand around the cane as I reposition myself. He cries out but still says nothing. Fresh bruises flower across his ass and back and I use my other hand to rake my nails across them. He shudders and lets out a groan. I move up his back and drape my arm over his shoulder.

"How are we doing?"

"Good." His hands twist to grab the cords holding him and pull on them. "I'm good."

"Mm, you sure?" I ask. Now that he's loosened up, maybe he'll start to answer my real questions. "Why did you want to stop?"

"I'm sorry."

"I know, and it's okay. It's more than okay. I just want to know why."

He apologizes again, so I gently tap the cane against a fresh bruise. He hisses and I move to strike a new spot. A thin red welt appears on his body. Strike after strike, I make art out of the crisscrossed red marks on his back. He lets out a deep breath when I pause in my strikes, but is still silent.

"Is something wrong, David?"

He shakes his head as an answer and I strike him harder. Right now I hate how strong he is, how much of a tolerance he's built to pain, and how much he bottles himself up when something matters. He grunts as he shifts. He curses before taking a deep breath and righting his body.

Why won't he talk to me? Is he hiding something? Is he angry? I might have to break him to get any answers out of him. He makes the right sounds and goes through the motions, but he's not with me. He's throwing a wall up.

"Talk to me!" I'm pleading at this point.

He won't let me in. "I love you. I'm sorry."

"Something else," I growl. "What's bothering you?"

"The weather was shit today," he grunts.

It's like he's testing me. I strike him again. Harder. He's talking about nonsense. I need to know what he's truly feeling. "Why won't you talk to me?" I take my frustration out on his back. This is what he wants. This is what he needs in order to open up. He silently takes the beating. It makes me hit him harder.

"Just tell me what's bothering you!" I yell. In the past, he would stonewall me for days. Part of me fears that it's going to happen again, is terrified that I've made it happen again. I turn the skin of his ass bright red and hit him again and again and again. I pour all of my frustration into him.

David suddenly lets out a broken sound and I still my hand.

He doesn't safeword, but this is over. He collapses against the restraints. Finally. He sobs. The dam has opened. He's completely boneless, relying on the restraints to hold him up. His head hangs to the side and his chest heaves with pants. I glance at my cane and then lower it. The limits have been pushed, I'm satisfied, and he has gone beyond what I thought he could. Maybe this can go further, maybe I can push him until he safewords and becomes even more of a desperate husk of a man, but there's no need. I'm satisfied.

I love this man with everything I am.

"That's enough now." My voice is soft and light. I uncuff his hands and they fall to his side as he sags on the floor. "I want to give you a bath."

He looks at me. Tear tracks mark his beautiful face. He nods slowly, like he's barely processing my words. "I'd like that." His voice is barely audible.

"Okay, come on." I pull him into my arms. He hugs me softly, and I bury my head into his neck. "I love you." I say it into every piece of skin my lips can reach with a kiss, and I pray that he can feel my love in all the ways I'm not able to convey with my words.

He's silent. I pull back and cup his face in my hands. David doesn't look angry, but he does look troubled. My thumb brushes over the hard prickly hair of his beard as I wipe his tears from his face. I touch his broad shoulders and then run my fingers down his arms to grab his hands.

I keep my eyes locked on his watery ones as I place tender kisses on his knuckles. He shuts his eyes tightly, and a fresh pair of tears race down his face. They fall off of his cheeks to land on his chest, and I pull on his arms gently to lead him out of the living room.

We take slow steps to the bathroom, and I let the praise flow from my lips and surround him. I rub his back to try and ground him. He sits in the tub and I fill it with warm water and scented oil. He leans back into it until his shoulders are submerged and his knees are fully bent.

I wish we had a bigger tub. If we did, he'd be able to fully stretch out and rest after everything. I lean over to kiss his forehead and run my fingers through his hair. He's quiet. His eyes are closed. I can't rush this. I lower my hands into the water to check the temperature and start slowly touching his skin. David doesn't say anything. I grab the small stool and sit next to him.

I murmur soft words to him, taking the time to do everything slowly. I pour water on his head and body with my hands. I massage him one limb at a time, slowly and carefully. I use my words as much as my fingers to loosen the tension in his body. He is perfect. He is more beautiful here, broken in the tub, than he was on our wedding day. The sounds of his broken moans mean more to me than his vows. The feeling of his angry, swelling skin under my fingers brings me more joy than our first kiss as Mr. and Mrs.. This is how he shows his love most—this is how I feel it.

Minutes later, when I start rubbing the skin under his knuckles, he turns his hand over to grab mine. He brings my hand to his lips and then kisses my wrist. "I love you."

"I love you so much." I smile at him as he glances from my wrist to my face.

David smiles in return then shifts in the tub, sitting upright and letting his legs soak in the water. I continue to massage his hands and he makes a soft happy sound when I finish.

"How are you feeling?" I ask a moment later, moving my attention to the front of his chest.

He cracks an eye open to look at me before closing it. "Sore." He twists his neck one way, then the other, filling the small room with the sound of his joints cracking. "That was a lot."

"Was it too much?" I ask. He shakes his head. "Why was it a lot today?"

"I don't know." David sighs. I let the silence fill the air, only interrupted by the sounds of the water moving against the tub. A minute passes, two. "I usually know that there is an ending. I can focus on that. It becomes a goal for me, a challenge that I can accomplish."

David picks a foot up and rests it on the side of the tub and sinks into it. I say nothing.

"I was in the middle of it all and I couldn't help but think: is this where you want me forever?" he continues, so quiet I have to strain to hear him. "Desperate like an animal, achingly hard but powerless. Caged and captured. I thought that's what you wanted. I thought this was my life now: just a toy for you, to be boxed away when you're done with me. I unlocked the cage, angry and ready to end it all, but then I realized I would be that. If I could do it, I'd do it forever for you. I love you so much, I do. Please don't throw me away." He shifts suddenly, spilling water out of the tub as his arms wrap around me tightly. He soaks my clothes, and the water splashes onto the bathroom floor

"I would never. Don't you know how much you mean to me?"

I yelp when David pulls me into the tub with him. The back of my knees knock painfully against the ceramic. He pulls me to his chest, and I try to wrap an arm around the back of his head to properly hug him back.

I tell him. I tell him about falling in love with him decades ago. I describe my nerves as I moved in with him way too fast. I confess the butterflies on our wedding day. I detail the ways I fell more in love with him because of his submission. I tell him about every single time he's made me tear up in joy. I kiss all the skin I can find as I confess to falling in love all over again during the last few months.

"I knew this would be hard for you, and you've been a dream. You've been so good for me. Even when you thought you broke my trust and grabbed the key, you were perfect. You've always been perfect."

David crushes my chest against his and my mouth against his and he kisses me until I can't breathe. His hand moves from my back to tangle in my hair, holding me in place for a second kiss, for a third and fourth. Endless open mouth kisses until all I can breathe is his love. I kiss him back until he starts laughing.

Giggles burst out of me. "What?"

"The bathroom is a mess." He continues to laugh, full bellied laughs that shake us both and send me into fits of giggles. "I'm sorry."

"You naughty boy!" I barely manage to get out through my giggles.

"I've made a mess of you, too." David finally releases his grip on me. My clothes are soaked. The easiest solution is to take them off. I toss them to the floor and he chuckles at the wet splat they make.

"Let's get out of here." I kiss him once more. "I'm ready to snuggle in bed."

"Me too."

After throwing a bunch of towels on the floor and wiping myself down, I dry him off. I'm slow and careful, gently wiping his shoulders and back and checking on the aftermath of the caning session. Angry colors darken his skin, but my eyes keep getting pulled to his scars. I trace the thin line a branch left on him when he fell out of a tree as a child. I kiss the small crater that a mole left behind after surgery.

I move to his hips, then his front. There's a thick line on his arm from a work injury, where a falling piece of wood sent him to the hospital. It's under the semi-permanent rash on his arm that only fades when he takes a vacation. Moving to his hands, I spot the jagged line on his finger from getting too close to a saw.

I kneel in front of him, gently wiping off his legs one at a time, and trace the line on his knee from a gutter he walked into. It's impossible to see, even as I wipe his feet, but how many small dots litter his feet from stepping on nails, or from blisters that turned into callouses?

David bears dozens of scars from his job. His job even ruined his shoulder.

Denial

"If I bear all of these scars for money, why wouldn't I want to bear a scar of love from you?"

I hated the words at the time he first said them, but now? My throat dries as I move to his flaccid cock. I dry it with the same care as the rest of him. I love every inch of this man.

I said I was disgusted with the idea, but that was a lie. I was scared. There was a single thought in the back of my mind, a terrible dreadful doubt I could never breathe life into: what if we didn't work out? If we ended our relationship, or if one of us died, the other could move on. A paper could be unsigned, a ring removed, but a permanent scar? Every moment he lives in that body would be a moment he walked around marked, owned—mine. Didn't this prove it? He gave me his mind; he gave me his heart; why shouldn't I take his body too? David has been mine since before I knew what it meant. He's been mine in every way and he will always be mine in every way.

It's an amazing gift, being able to fall in love with him all over again through this process. When I give him permission to get into bed, I give him a long and sweet kiss.

"You're my everything," I tell him in between kisses.

"You're my all." David cups my cheek in his hand and his eyes are as warm as the beach we splashed around in during our honeymoon.

In the morning, I jerk him off nice and slow. No tricks or surprises today. David's done enough to deserve something nice and easy. He relaxes into the bed and I take him right to the edge, as normal, except I don't stop when his cock pulses in my hand.

"N—no." His hips jerk backwards and away from me as his eyes shoot open. Panic fills his eyes. "Mistress, I'm too close."

I follow him as he sits up against the headboard, and I resume stroking him. "Easy love, I've got you. I want you to come for me."

David trembles under my hand but doesn't move away. "Believe in me. I can go longer. I can make you proud." He shakes his head, trying to stop this from being over.

"I'm already proud of you." I kiss him, but he only tenses his body in response.

"This doesn't have to be the end. I can do this."

"I want it to be." My voice is soft as I continue to slowly stroke his cock. I could force him to come with a few hard and fast strokes, but I want him to enjoy it after all of this time. He needs to know that he deserves this. "I'm proud of you for lasting this long, but—"

"I don't." He puts his hand on my arm, but doesn't pull me away from him.

"You don't?"

"I can do this," he repeats. The determination in his voice mixes with desperation. Is he trying to convince himself? My motions slow but don't stop. "I don't want this to be *over*." His voice breaks. The rawness surprises me, and I stop to look at him.

"Why don't you want to come?"

"We've been so happy." He hides his head in my shoulder. "We've been finding time for this, and the dates, and you're glowing. I've never seen you so happy."

My throat dries. I lean back so that he can't hide from me. His eyes shine with moisture. He looks down, but I lift his chin so he has to meet my eyes. He's been feeling exactly what I have, hasn't he? It wasn't just the denial for me either: it was the attention. It was his devotion.

"I told you that I was falling for you all over again." My eyes burn. I wipe my tears away before they can fall.

"I think I forgot," he admits, catching a tear with his hand as he pushes my hair out of my face. "I forgot how much your smile means to me; how I would do anything to put it there, to keep it there."

My eyes squeeze shut and a shuddering breath gets caught in my throat. "I forgot, too." I choke out the words.

He pulls me into his chest and rubs his hand up and down my back. "If this cage brought us back to *this*, if missing a few orgasms brought back this much happiness…"

"No." I shake my head against his shoulder. "It wasn't just the cage." It was me. I changed my attitude towards everything, and it did all of this. I wanted a new challenge, new excitement, without realizing that what I really wanted was this.

"I don't want to give this up." He pulls me into his lap. "I don't know how we lost our spark, but its back, and I'm not losing it again."

"Never." I finally meet his eyes. Slowly, I wipe away the tears on his face, and then we're kissing. The slow gentle kiss sets me on fire, but not the fire of a quick spark. The fire of embers. A quick breeze reigniting coals. He hugs me tighter as I run my fingers through his hair softly.

"I won't forget," I promise as I pull back, kissing his forehead, his cheek, his nose.

"I won't let you." David dips down to kiss my chin, my throat, my shoulder. I pull my shirt over my head and he takes a nipple into his mouth and squeezes my ass.

"You were a monster with the timer." I whimper as he turns, laying me down on the bed. His hand commands my skin, and goosebumps race up to meet him as I arch into his touch. He trails his hand down my side and tugs my panties off.

He kisses down my stomach. "I liked the challenge." He opens my thighs for him. It's enough to make me moan as he wraps his hand around my ankle. "You were so confident, so wanton, it was easier to make you come when you already worked yourself up."

"You failed," I tease, but I don't have enough breath to put any weight behind it.

He hums and slides under my leg, hiking my thigh over his shoulder. His hot breath moves up my thigh as he moves closer to my pussy. He leaves a trail of open mouthed kisses on one thigh, and moves on to the other.

"You were so happy at the Playhouse."

I slide my fingers across the top of his head as he kisses my clit. "I—ah—I loved seeing your emotions fight for control of your face."

"Was that all?" He slides a finger into me. I'm already so wet that he chuckles before adding a second. "I thought you liked seeing me get fucked."

"Alex—" I cut off in a moan as he pumps me and licks me at once. I buck, but he's already captured my leg, and I go nowhere. "David. *David.* David," I chant as he perfectly works me into a frenzy.

"Much better." He sucks, and that's all it takes. I clench around his fingers as I push his head into my pussy, and he's laughing even as he works me through my orgasm.

"Hey," I say, in a daze, as I look at the ceiling. He pulls his fingers out of me and licks them clean. My hand falls to the bed as he sits up. "I was supposed to make you come."

"Were you?" He crawls over me, hiking my leg up as he settles between my legs. Before I can respond, he captures my lips in a kiss and rolls his hips into mine.

On the third roll, his cock finally slides into me, and I let out a muffled moan that he swallows. He rocks into me slowly, and it's like payback for all I've done to him these past few months. I kiss him like I never will again, like I only have a few minutes to memorize how he kisses. Slow kisses build into fast sloppy ones. They slow again.

My world narrows into the man in front of me. Our kiss breaks and he stares down into my eyes as he keeps his slow pace. Somehow its more intimate this way. My orgasm builds, and I don't want to do it alone. I hold his eyes with a soft smile. I want to see him fall apart.

"Will you come for me?"

He arches a brow. "What if I say no?"

"You never say no to me," I laugh, and he dips down to kiss me again.

"Maybe I will one day."

"Please, David." Have I ever begged this man for anything before? "Please."

"Iris—" He thrusts again and it's over.

He yells as he comes, but his body moves as if he's forgotten how. His face scrunches like he's in pain. Tears slip out of the corner of his eyes and he screams out. His body jerks in bed as hot spurts of cum shoot out of his cock and into me. I'd forgotten how satisfying it feels. It throbs over and over as he continues to come uncontrollably. I clench around him and he gasps. Does it hurt? Has he forgotten how I feel when we come together? Maybe he's coming more than once.

"We'll keep the spark," I promise as he pulls out. He kisses down my chest and makes his way down my stomach.

"We'd better." He blows a raspberry into my belly button.

I squeal, pushing him away and bursting into laughter. David cracks up a second later and falls on to the bed next to me. "Shower?"

"We're a mess." The corner of his lips turn up. "Come on." David grabs my hand and leads me to the bathroom.

His cage sits on the bathroom sink, clean and dry. I pick it up and turn it over in my hands. Such a little thing. Such power. I shake my head and place the cage back in its spot in the cabinet, where it will stay until David takes it out. It may stay forever, but I don't mind if it does.

Epilogue – Mine

My phone chirps with a message as David empties half the box of cereal into his bowl. He arches his brows as I turn the phone over to check it. *Finally!* Thorn is the expert on everything ink and design, so I shouldn't be surprised that it's perfect. I should have been waiting months for this, but Thorn cleared everything off the table for us. No matter what I say, I think he'll always feel indebted to us.

"Should I be worried?" David is on the high of regular orgasms again. I doubt much could worry him at the moment. I shake my head and laugh as I start typing a response. David shakes his head, but his smile grows into a grin as he munches away. "Okay, now I'm worried."

"You should keep your evening free." I wink. "We've been invited to Thorn's shop tonight and I don't think you'll want to miss it."

David's spoon clatters into the bowl. His widening eyes fill with the shine of hope as he waits for me to clarify, to pull the rug out on his dreams, but that's not what's happening.

"You mean…" His grin morphs into something else entirely. It lights up his entire face and takes twenty years off of it. My heart swells at the sight. He drums his hands on the table. "What changed your mind?"

"You did."

"We haven't talked about this in months."

"You gave me everything." I meet his gaze. He begged to stay locked up; he was willing to be nothing but an animal for me. His submission is precious to me, almost as precious as he is, and though the idea of owning him so completely once scared me, it doesn't anymore.

David waits for more of an explanation.

"You gave me *everything*," I stress. How can I put it into words in any other way?

He scoffs. "All these years, and *that's* what it took? Do I get to see it?"

Denial

I pull up the picture and contemplate the lines that will decorate David until we rot together in the ground. Instead of the bent and twisted metal I once thought I would need, a thick pen-like tool sits on the table in its packaging. He'll be able to draw the burn on to David, and then I'll be able to trace it on his thigh every time I lay between his legs to tease him. I'll be able to touch it casually when we are out to eat. He'll see it if he jerks off or when he showers. "Do you want to see it?"

"I trust you." David's eyes drop to my phone. "I want to see it, but if part of it is not showing me, I won't look."

I slide the phone over to him. "I like it better when you walk in with both eyes open."

Will he like it? I kept it simple, but there's no way to brush it off as anything other than a brand. The soft inside of his thigh will always be mine. Even when I share him, I'll always be right there as a physical reminder. He ducks his head as he zooms in on the picture.

Does he hate it? Thorn could always make a new design for us. He might curse me out but he'd make a new one in his 'own damn time' and then we could reschedule. I cross my arms to prevent my nails from drumming on the counter.

"Tonight?" His voice is barely a whisper. Heat prickles the back of my neck. Am I moving too soon? His hand tightens around the phone as his tongue wets his lips. He clears his throat but doesn't look up. "I get to wear this tonight?"

"You'll wear it forever."

He places the phone face down on the table. "I'm not trying to say no to a good thing. I've wanted this for years."

It sounds like he's about to say no.

David sighs and taps the phone. "You were against this for a long time. You yelled at me the last time I brought it up. Do you really want this or is this just because of last weekend?"

"I want to know you're mine in the dark," I blurt.

He doesn't respond to that.

Heat rises to my cheeks. "All the reasons I have against it don't seem to mean as much anymore. I have you, and I'll always have you. Your love is branded in my heart, and it's never going to leave me. I can only imagine it's the same for you."

"Of course, it is." David places his hand over mine and rubs my knuckles.

I turn our hands over and trace the scars on his wrist from his surgery. "If you want that brand on the surface, then

I want to give it to you. I needed time to think about it. I needed to see that it was more than a passing interest in a new kink. I needed to want it too."

"Do you?"

…for as long as you both shall live?

"I do."

"I'd be remiss if I didn't ask. Are you both completely, totally, one hundred percent sure?"

"Yes." David nods. "I don't want to wait another minute."

Thorn's lips twitch up on one side. "Well, you will. There's a lot to get through before I lay a hand on you." Thorn takes his time explaining the process in more detail than he had before to either of us. He shows us the thermocautery pen and explains how it operates at 1200 degrees Celsius, killing the nerves in the area. Somehow, it'll hurt more after he's done than it will during the process. A lot of it is similar to a tattoo, except he's burning the skin instead of inking it.

The worst part will be the long healing period. The skin will blister and hurt. The consent documents are thick. The aftercare packet is thicker. There's also an anti-care packet, which details how to agitate the scars to make them thicker and raise them. Thorn mentioned all of this before, but seeing it written out is sobering. There's so much here, and none of it can be taken back.

David glows with excitement as he signs the papers. He'd glowed the same way when he'd signed our marriage license. Thorn shoves them in a drawer as he taps the tattooing chair. "Alright then. Take your pants off."

Thorn wheels his station over and puts on blue gloves. "Last chance." He hums as he shaves the inside of David's thigh. I pull a chair next to David.

"I'm all in." David's hand squeezes mine. His thumb moves up and down the back of my hand, but his eyes never leave Thorn. Nerves twist in my stomach. Thorn places the stencil on David's thigh and my nerves burst into anticipation and arousal. Those thin purple lines will soon be thick, raised white scars. My mouth dries. I lift David's hand to my lips and kiss his fingers. David's eyes meet mine and they somehow look like molten gold in the light.

Mine.

"Grab whatever you have to grab, this is going to hurt more than anything you've done before." Thorn pins David's thigh between the chair and his knee. He turns the pen on, and waits for David's go ahead.

David's skin sizzles immediately, and he clenches my hand so tightly I wince. The air fills with the scent of burnt skin, and instead of twisting my nose at the foul smell, I can't help but to inhale.

"Oh, that hurts!" David curses. "Fuck!"

My bones shift under the pressure, but I barely feel it. How much pain is he in? No matter how much it is, it's all for me. The sick smell in the air is mine. David is burning his love for me in his thigh, carving a space for no one but me that will never fade.

"Let me know if you need to stop." Thorn's voice is gentle and his hands are precise, but David howls like he's being flayed alive.

Maybe it *feels* like he's being flayed alive. He tosses his head back into the chair and tears roll down his cheek. I'd stand and lick them off of his face if I could without moving everything. His tears leave dark droplets on his shirt that would feel like a waste, except they are all for me too.

The skin looks red and raw under Thorn's gloves, and the fiery orange glow of the pen leaves another line behind.

Suddenly, words erupt from me. Praise erupts from me. Love confessions that would make a fairytale blush, and vows of devotion that would make a priest sweat. I love this man to the end and back. I will stand with him against any and everything. We belong to each other. There is nothing in this world that will ever mean more to me than his love. No gift greater than his submission. He makes me brave and beautiful, he lifts me to heights unknown, and he loves me with a love that is more than love. Tears cloud my eyes.

He breaks me.

I lay any stupid stubborn pride at his feet. My insecurities vanish into the ether. If everything that I am is everything that he needs, then I must be *everything*. He is me. I am him. His devotion to me is unmatched by the forces around us, and my devotion to him is as vast as the universe—

"I can't," David croaks. "Parachute." The pen clicks off and my voice stops. David goes limp against the chair and Thorn rolls away to grab the wrap.

"Perfect timing." Thorn's voice is soft. "You're done. You're branded."

I kiss every inch of David's hand. He finally opens his eyes. "I am?"

"Take a picture, Iris. It won't look like this again for months."

The picture I want most, the memory I want to cherish the most, is David's face. It's a masterpiece of tears and pain, of love and devotion, and it's all mine. I grab my phone and take pictures of everything. David is beautiful, the brand is beautiful, and even if they weren't, what matters most is that they are mine.

Forever and always, in every possible way.

It takes six months for the scars to heal enough that Thorn clears sexual activities, and after that it only takes David three months to toss the cage on the bed again. I slowly rake my eyes over his naked body but all I can see is my brand on his thigh and the smile on his face.

"Are you sure? I may actually break you this time."

He kneels. "As it pleases you, Mistress."

The End

Author's note

Orgasm denial was one of the first kinks I explored writing about, when all I had were short stories and dreams of writing books. It has always been one of my favorites and I'm so happy I was able to come up with a novella idea that captures what I enjoy best about it.

I think it has a bit of a bad reputation, that its cruel to do to a partner or is should only be done as part of edging for a bigger orgasm, but when I focus in on the details about it I don't see that at all. You really have to know your partner to bring them to the edge without tipping over, you really have to trust your partner not to 'finish the job' when you aren't around, and there's a rush of power knowing that they are waiting, and wanting, and dangling over the edge for you. On the other hand, giving that control over creates a desperation that can feel feral, changes the purpose of every intimate interaction, and (if done right) basks you in attention, the safe feeling of being owned and kept, and a challenge unlike most others.

For Iris and David, orgasm denial was a tool used to help them refocus on each other at a time where it was growing easy to get stuck in a routine. Young love and new love is always going to be fun to write about, but deepening love, or returning to it, was something I wanted to explore, and an older couple that had been married forever but was losing that spark felt perfect.

If you enjoyed this story, please leave a rating or review. It helps small authors like me get seen, and helps readers like you decide to give it a chance.

I currently have plans for bondage and primal play to join the Kinkotica series, but please, if there are kinks you want to see, reach out! I love engagement and conversations with my readers. For information on my work and releases, feel free to check out AllyMarr.com or follow me on Instagram or Threads at Ally_Marr_.

Also by Ally Marr:

Desire for Dominance:

"Let me worship you, please. I'd be such a good boy for you."

It doesn't take a rocket scientist to figure out relationships, but when Lily—an actual rocket engineer—decides to try something new, neither relationships nor rocket science prove to be easy. When her best friend Tala drags her to the local swinging club, Lily walks straight into a dungeon filled with leather, kinksters, and Mark.

Mark stretches on the cross, held by leather cuffs on his wrists and ankles, but Lily is the one that's bound. He's gorgeous, driven, and eager to show her the ropes. There's only one problem: Lily is so new to the scene she's not even sure what "the scene" is, let alone how to be a domme in one. He awakens her desire for dominance, but is it enough to satisfy the darkest of his needs?

https://mybook.to/Ay3X2u

Milton Keynes UK
Ingram Content Group UK Ltd.
UKHW011349280624
444890UK00030B/203

9 798988 281122